Coastal Rescue

COASTAL RESCUE

Preserving Our Seashores

by
CHRISTINA G. MILLER
and
LOUISE A. BERRY

Illustrated with photographs and diagrams

Atheneum   1989   New York

The directions for making a wave tank are based on material developed by Education Development Center, Newton, Massachusetts, part of an exhibit designed by Cambridge Seven Associates, Inc., Cambridge, Massachusetts, for the New England Aquarium in 1969, and are used with permission.

The quote on page 72 is from *Guide to Cape Cod; Based on Cape Cod by Henry David Thoreau,* ed. by Alexander B. Adams. New York: The Devin-Adair Company, 1962, p. 89.

Copyright © 1989 by Christina G. Miller and Louise A. Berry
All rights reserved.

ATHENEUM
MACMILLAN PUBLISHING COMPANY
866 Third Avenue, New York, NY 10022
Collier Macmillan Canada, Inc.
First Edition   Printed in the United States of America
10 9 8 7 6 5 4 3 2 1

Library of Congress Cataloging-in-Publication Data
Miller, Christina G.
Coastal rescue/by Christina G. Miller and Louise A. Berry;
illustrated with photographs and diagrams. p. cm. Bibliography: p. Includes index.
Summary: Examines different types of coasts; how they are shaped by nature; how the development of coasts has destroyed plant and animal life, beaches, and marshes; and ways to use coasts' valuable resources and still preserve them.
ISBN 0–689–31288–1
1. Coastal zone management—United States—Juvenile literature. 2. Shore protection—United States—Juvenile literature. 3. Marine pollution—United States—Juvenile literature. [1. Coastal zone management. 2. Shore protection. 3. Marine pollution. 4. Coasts.]
I. Berry, Louise A. II. Title. HT392.M54 1989
333.91'7'0973—dc19 88-27520 CIP AC

Photo credits: Massachusetts Coastal Zone Management: 2, 8b, 11, 34–35, 41, 42, 45, 50, 82, 86, 88   Alison Shaw: xiii, 10, 14, 36–37, 81, 100   Bernie Yokel: 3, 93, 94–95 M. C. Wallo Photography: 4–5, 24–25   Sarah Marshall: 6, 8a, 59   Louise A. Berry: 30   Courtesy of National Park Service, Gateway National Recreation Area, Sandy Hook Unit: 38, 70–71, 106   San Diego Historical Society—Ticor Collection: 44a and b   Carol Lundeen: 46–47   NASA: 53   Virginia Institute of Marine Science: 55, 85   Bob Walker—SF Bay: 61   David Twichell: 72–73, 103   Save the Bay, Providence, RI: 66   Rhode Island Division Fish and Wildlife: 65   Scott Melvin, Mass. Div. of Fisheries and Wildlife: 75   Donald L. Rheem II: 79   Walter S. Silver: 108.

Dedicated to the survival of Canis rufus

ACKNOWLEDGMENTS

We would like to thank the following people for being valuable resources to us as we researched material for this book:

Dr. K. O. Emery
Department of Geology and Geophysics
Woods Hole Oceanographic Institution

Ms. Barbara Fegan
Coastal Specialist
League of Women Voters of Massachusetts

Mr. P. Michael Payne
Manomet Bird Observatory
Manomet, Massachusetts

Dr. Bernard Yokel
President
Florida Audubon Society

CONTENTS

1
A Visit to the Coast

HE coast is the area between land and sea. It is the last frontier before the watery ocean wilderness that covers two-thirds of planet Earth. Just as a fender protects a car, the coastal zone acts like a bumper to protect the land from the sea. It keeps the ocean away from higher land by absorbing the energy of waves.

In the slightly more than three and one-half centuries since the Pilgrims came to America, people have caused vast changes in the coast. As a small, struggling colony grew into a great nation, the land, water, air, plants, animals, and non-living things that make up the coastal *environment* were greatly affected. Much of the "natural coast" upon which the *Mayflower* voyagers set foot has gradually been transformed into a "developed coast."

Lighthouse on a rocky New England coast.

Today about 70 percent of the population of the United States lives within fifty miles of the ocean. High-rise condominiums and hotels, marinas, commercial fishing wharves, sewage treatment plants, oil refineries, nuclear power plants, paved parking lots, amusement parks, and houses built on shifting sands are all part of our developed coast. We have not always used the natural resources of the coast wisely. Therefore, many citizens and scientists now believe that this very special place will require greater understanding and care if it is to be preserved for future generations.

Let's take an imaginary trip in a small plane to look at the many widely different kinds of coasts found in the continental United States. Taking off in the Northeast, we see the jagged, island-strewn, rocky coast of Maine. Dense evergreen forests grow to where rocky cliffs meet the sea. Along the southern

New England and mid-Atlantic coast, we see tall green grass swaying in low wetlands called *salt marshes,* woods of shrubby scrub oak and pine, and sandy beaches. Along the Florida coast, swamps of mangrove trees, pinkish white coral sand beaches, and the semitropical Everglades come into view.

The coast of the Gulf of Mexico varies from the shell-strewn beaches of the west coast of Florida to shallow areas off Texas and Louisiana, where rivers deposit *silt* composed of fine particles of sand, dirt, clay, and other material. Along the California coast we see high cliffs pounded by crashing surf. Those steep cliffs continue with a scattering of beaches northwest to the coast of Oregon and Washington. Here we see mountains that seem to plunge toward the sea. If we were to fly on to

Aerial view of mangrove swamps along the Florida coast.

When the incoming tide reaches this sand castle, it will topple.

Alaska, we would see spectacular ice caps, called *glaciers,* along its rocky coast.

The shape of the coast is constantly being altered by the forces of nature. Wind, waves, tides, currents, and weather move the rocks, sand, pebbles, soil, and mud of which continents are made and sculpt the coast into new forms. By comparing old and recent maps of the same coastal area, we can see changes in the land that borders the sea. In addition, some

islands may be drowning, while in other places new beaches may be forming. For billions of years nature has shaped and reshaped the coast by pounding, pulling, and pushing the shore. Beaches and even islands must move in order to stay healthy. People want coastal land they have purchased and houses they have built to be permanent, but coasts resist efforts to be "stabilized." They are in a constant state of change.

Have you ever built a sand castle on the hard, wet sand at

low tide? When the tide turned, the incoming waves nibbled away at the base of the castle. Even encircling it with rocks and digging a channel to route the water away protected it only temporarily. If there was surf, a breaker toppled the castle when the incoming tide reached it. Whether calm seas or rough, not a trace of the castle remained later that same day.

Sometimes large *seawalls* are built of concrete or boulders to protect the shore from stormy seas and save beachfront property. But, in constructing seawalls, bulldozers often re-

A seawall at Sandy Hook, New Jersey.

move sand *dunes*—mounds or ridges of sand piled up by wind, which are natural storm barriers. Without the dunes, *erosion,* a wearing or washing away, actually increases. Over time the sand that was once on the beach is carried out to sea, leaving a rocky shore behind. Some places where the beaches are becoming "beachless" are Miami Beach, Florida; Galveston, Texas; and Atlantic City, New Jersey.

Sandy parts of the 5,100-mile coastline of the lower forty-eight states are growing narrower each year. Mission Beach, near San Diego, California, is now referred to as "Missing Beach" because it has disappeared under the waves. In 1976 the state of California passed a law requiring communities located in the coastal zone to preserve, protect, and restore coastal resources for the future. Plans for proposed new buildings, ports, power plants, or other projects must take into account the effect they will have on the coast.

The challenge in taking care of the coast lies in finding the right balance among all of the various ways we can use the valuable coastal resources and still preserve them. The first step in becoming a modern "coast guardian," or one who protects the coast, is to develop "coast awareness."

If you were to spend a summer on Cape Cod, Massachusetts, for example, older people would tell you that many changes had occurred there in their lifetimes. During July and August, along the congested Cape highways, exhaust fumes mingle with the salt air. Some country roads formerly suitable for walking and bicycling have now been widened to accommodate the heavy traffic. Long lines of cars loaded down with bicycles, umbrella strollers, groceries, suitcases, tennis rackets, and camping gear barely move. In the place of rustic clam shacks and guest houses you are likely to see fast-food chain restau-

Sand dunes have been bulldozed so that houses, stores, and roads can be built.

rants and large, modern motels with swimming pools. Supermarkets, drugstores, appliance and furniture stores, service stations, parking lots, souvenir shops, and video rental stores now stand where once there were salt marshes and fields of grass. Some Cape Cod residents are now debating how to protect the Cape from further development and thereby preserve its natural beauty.

If growth continues, the supply of fresh water may not be adequate. In the last fifteen years, the year-round population of Cape Cod has nearly doubled. Its towns are no longer "ghost towns" in the winter. Existing *sewage* treatment plants are a major source of *pollution* because they are not equipped to treat the amount of *wastewater* discharged from the increasing numbers of homes and businesses. Clamming is prohibited in some places because the salt water is impure. Eating clams, oysters, and other *shellfish* taken from polluted water can cause illness.

Many parts of Cape Cod are still pure enough for clamming. Clams and other shellfish are some of the *natural resources* of the coast. Natural resources are the living and nonliving things found in nature that are valuable or necessary to people. Just a few years ago, quahogs, a kind of clam, were so plentiful on Cape Cod that overdigging occurred. People took more than they needed and either threw the quahogs in the garbage or used them to bait lobster traps. So many of those clams were harvested that in recent years the supply has dwindled.

Sandy beaches are natural resources that have also been harmed by people's misuse. Many beaches are crowded and noisy in the summer. Radios blare, motorboats tow water skiers, and broken bottles and food wrappers are discarded in the sand. Seawalls built on Cape Cod actually may cause sand to be washed out to sea. In place of the sand are small rocks and pebbles that hurt bare feet. Large signs at the parking lots next to many beaches read Help Control Erosion—Keep Off Dunes. Use Walkways. Here the dunes are surrounded with snow fencing used to retain the sand rather than hold back snow. Tall clumps of beach grass grow on top of the imprisoned dunes. The paths between the snow fencing lead from the parking lot to the beach to keep people from wearing down the dunes.

On the beach you might encounter the horseshoe crab, one of nature's most primitive yet most successful animals. The horseshoe crab is a species that has existed on Earth for more than 300 million years. It has survived since before the time of the dinosaurs. In the water, a horseshoe crab looks like a brownish black rock. It has a long, swordlike tail and a soft

Harvesting shellfish in coastal waters.

Snow fencing protects these sand dunes.

underside with five pairs of wriggling legs. The pointed tail spike is not a stinger. Rather, the horseshoe crab uses it as a lever to right itself, should the crab find itself upside down. In contrast to most other animals, the horseshoe crab you might meet today looks much the same as its prehistoric ancestors.

If you want to experience the kind of natural coast where horseshoe crabs lived millions of years ago, perhaps you can visit a National Seashore. These areas are protected from development and are part of the National Park System. National Seashores belong to all of the citizens of the United States; they are not owned by any one person or town or state. At each visitor center, National Park rangers talk about the plants and animals of the coast. They explain that the vast stretches of seemingly uninhabited sand dunes, marshes, meadows, and woods are actually teeming with life that a keen observer can discover. To walk the Cape Cod National Seashore, with its dense forests, sandy beaches, mud flats, salt marshes, swamps, and dunes, is to become acquainted with the kind of coast that greeted the Pilgrims when they arrived in the New World.

2
Natural Architects of the Coast

~~~~~~~~

THE seashore is at once both familiar and foreign. We are mystified by the coast, which belongs neither to land nor sea completely. Coastal waves, tides, currents, and winds provide an ever-changing land- and seascape.

One sure way of getting to know our natural coastlines would be to do as Henry Beston did in 1926. This little-known writer from Quincy, Massachusetts, was a naturalist and wanted to get to know the coast more intimately than he could as an occasional visitor. He built a very small house facing the Atlantic Ocean at the top of a sand dune on Eastham Beach on Cape Cod.

The house consisted of a kitchen/living room and a bedroom. A brick fireplace built into the wall between the two

rooms provided heat, and a two-burner oil stove was used for cooking. A well pipe driven through the kitchen floor and into the sand dune tapped into fresh water. With a hand-operated pump, the pipe brought the water to the kitchen sink.

The house had no other indoor plumbing. Lanterns, candles, and the fireplace were the only sources of light. Ten windows in the tiny house looked out onto *moors,* meadows, salt marshes, and sea. One window faced Nauset Light to the north. Although Beston had intended to live this lonely existence only for a few weeks, he became so fascinated with the mysteries of the coast that he lived in his little house an entire year.

Beston's account of a year on the beach was published in the book *The Outermost House,* which became a nature classic still widely read today. He experienced every aspect of the beach on which he lived. He studied its birds, insects, and plants. He listened to the sounds of the beach—the waves, the wind, the rain. He watched the changing panorama of colors as morning turned to noon and then to evening and as the seasons changed. He delighted in the smells of the sea—the crisp, salty air, the delicate fragrance of wildflowers, and the dank odor of the seaweed decaying on the beach.

Beston lived by the rhythms of nature. The roar of the surf at midnight seemed more powerful than the breaking surf of the daylight hours. With the arrival of winter, the beach seemed almost lifeless, except for the gulls. Not only were sunbathers gone, but also the animals and insects seemed to have "disappeared into the chill air." The beach was cold and desolate. Many days the sky was overcast, and the sea turned a forbidding greenish black. Some nights were so foggy that

Sunrise over a deserted beach.

even Nauset Light two miles away could not penetrate the darkness. To walk on the beach on such a night was to feel enveloped by total blackness. On a clear night, however, the twinkling stars overhead made one feel a renewed sense of being a small part of the immense universe. With the arrival of a northeast storm, sleet rattled against the windows of the little house and whitecaps churned in the wild sea.

Perhaps you have seen movies showing waves pounding rocky coastlines, or maybe on television you have watched surfers gracefully riding the smooth surface of a huge wave. You may also have seen paintings of the ocean in which water was so still that it looked like a mirror reflecting the sky. Depending on the height and strength of waves, the ocean can seem as calm as a reflecting pool or as ferocious as a raging river.

When wind travels over water, it drags the water surface with it, creating waves. You can see how that happens by blowing through a straw, holding the end of it just above water level in the glass. The pressure of the moving air in your breath causes ripples in the water similar to the way that wind forms waves in the sea. The faster the wind, and the longer and farther it blows, the bigger the waves.

Wind is the result of the uneven heating of the air surrounding our planet. The sun does not warm all parts of the earth equally. As the air is heated by the sun, it rises, and cooler air moves in to take its place.

Most waves are formed by gusty winds blowing over a broad expanse of water. Several sets of waves traveling in different directions are sometimes present at the same time. When that occurs, we say the sea is "choppy." The height of waves is determined by the length of time the wind blows, its speed, and

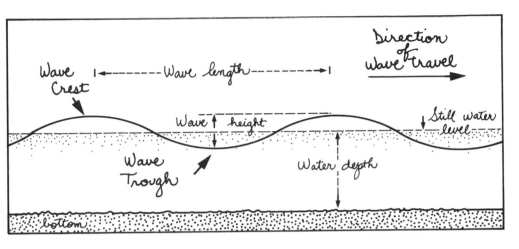

How a wave is measured.

the distance the wind has traveled across water. The highest point of a wave is called its crest, and waves higher than twenty-five feet are unusual. Storm winds, though, can produce waves as high as fifty feet; even an occasional wave more than one hundred feet tall has been recorded. That is about as tall as a seven-story building.

The lowest point of a wave is called the trough. The length of a wave is the horizontal distance between one crest and the next one. When wave height is about one-seventh the length, the crest moves faster than the rest of the wave, and it spills over in front. That is called a whitecap. A whitecap occurs when wind speed is about fifteen miles per hour or more.

The water in a wave moves, although it does not advance. If you have ever watched waves on the ocean surface, it may look to you as if water is traveling from one place to another, but that is not so. If you keep your eye on a piece of seaweed or a stick floating on the water, you will see it rise and fall as the wave passes, but the motion of the wave will not cause the stick to move toward shore. To understand the motion of a wave, tie a rope to a tree trunk. Now hold the free end of the rope and move it up and down so waves move through it. You will see them reach the tree, but the rope will not have moved any closer toward the tree.

In a similar way, each water particle moves in a circle and returns to almost its exact position. When a wave enters shallow water, the water particles can no longer move in a complete circle. That shortens the length of the wave and increases its height. The wave gets so high that it topples forward, or "breaks." When that happens, the water in the wave actually does advance, sending forth a rush of water onto the shore.

While wind is the cause of most ocean waves, you probably can think of other ways that waves are made. For example, you can throw a stone into water and see circles of small waves move out from where the pebble landed. The movement of a powerboat can also cause waves that make your raft bob up and down as you float in the water.

The study of waves has been going on for almost five thousand years. Perhaps you have seen a wave tank. The Museum of Science in Boston, Massachusetts, has a ninety-foot-long wave tank, which holds 2,693 gallons of water. The exhibit allows visitors to see a cross-sectional view of waves traveling through the water and breaking on a sloping surface, like a beach.

You can easily make a small wave tank of your own. You will need:

Mineral oil or castor oil (available at drugstores)
cold water

a tall, narrow glass jar
blue food coloring

Directions:
1. Fill ⅓ of the jar with cold water.
2. Add a few drops of blue coloring. Swirl the jar to mix the color.
3. Fill the jar to the top with oil.
4. Screw the cover on tightly.
5. Hold the jar horizontally and move it gently back and forth to see the motion of the waves.

Like waves, most ocean *currents* are powered by the wind. Currents are parts of the ocean that move continuously in one direction. They flow like huge rivers moving millions of gallons of salt water through the oceans. Despite the fact that ocean currents move over such long distances, these large volumes of water keep a fairly steady temperature. Therefore, currents affect the coastlines that they are near. Winds blowing off a warm sea bring milder weather to the coast. A cold current near the shore can make coastlines cooler than inland areas. Much of the seafloor is covered with a layer of food, or *nutrients,* resulting from the decay of dead plants and animals. Some currents bring those nutrients from the depths of the ocean to the surface where they create rich feeding areas for sea animals.

Although there are many currents in Earth's oceans, two primary systems affect coastal areas of the United States: the warm Gulf Stream in the Atlantic Ocean and the cold California current in the Pacific Ocean. Both of these currents originate because of the same wind system—the trade winds.

The Gulf Stream begins near the equator in the western

Caribbean, where it is hot all year long. As the air in that area rises, cool air from the north and south rushes in to take its place. Because of the rotation of Earth on its axis to the east, the air does not move in a direct line toward the equator. Instead, it blows southwest and northwest. That wind pattern, which moves the air near the equator from east to west, is called the trade winds. The trade winds were given their name because they blow steadily and therefore helped the sailing ships that brought goods from Europe to America or from America to Asia.

The westward-blowing trade winds start to pull the surface water along with them. The current of the Gulf Stream flows into the Gulf of Mexico and around the tip of Florida and then north along the East Coast to Cape Cod. It carries north water that is from eleven to eighteen degrees Fahrenheit (six to ten degrees centigrade) warmer than surrounding water. As the Gulf Stream nears Cape Cod, it travels northeast until it is off

Major ocean currents of North America.

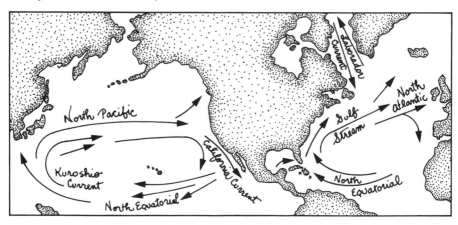

the coast of Newfoundland. There it meets the chill Labrador current, and some mixing of warm and cold water occurs. Because the Gulf Stream does not reach areas in the United States that are north of Cape Cod, waters there are much colder.

The California current results from the North Equatorial current, which is the largest current in the world. It moves water 9,000 miles from Panama westward to the Philippine Islands. There it turns north, becoming the warm Kuroshio current, which travels along the coast of Japan. The North Pacific current is formed from warm water from the Kuroshio current and cold water from the frigid northern part of the Pacific Ocean near the coast of Alaska. As that current approaches the West Coast of North America, much of the cooled water becomes the cold California current, which flows southward along the West Coast of the United States on its journey toward the equator. There it once again becomes part of the North Equatorial current.

Those current systems are only a few of the many surface currents that exist in the oceans of Earth. Some places also have deep water currents that exist beneath surface currents and may even run in opposite directions to them. Such a current exists south of Point Conception in California. Here the California countercurrent, a deep undercurrent, brings tropical water northward from Baja, California. That warms Southern California coastal areas. Countercurrents are usually caused, not by the wind, but by differences in the temperature or saltiness of ocean waters.

When water is warmed near the equator, it becomes lighter than water cooled by ice and freezing temperatures near the poles. Just as with air, warmer water tends to rise, and cooler water sinks. Those movements of warm and cold water result in currents at different depths below the surface.

The salt content, or *salinity,* of seawater is influenced by the inflow of fresh water from rivers, melting snow, rainfall, and by evaporation. In some warm seas, such as the Red Sea, Persian Gulf, and the Mediterranean Sea, so much evaporation occurs that the water has a high salt content. In other areas, a great deal of rain or melting snow dilutes the concentration of salt in the water. When waters with different salinities meet, the salty water, which is heavier, sinks to the bottom, and fresher water flows in above it, creating a current.

While currents move water in a certain direction, tides are the periodic rise and fall of the waters of the ocean. If you are walking along the beach at high tide, you may notice that the shoreline that was dotted with sand castles only a few hours earlier is now underwater. Much of the beach has been covered by the advancing sea, leaving only a narrow ribbon of sand on which you can put your beach towel.

The height of the tides is influenced by three factors: the *gravitational* pull of the Moon and the Sun, the depth of the ocean and shape of the shore, and the time it takes for the large amount of water in the oceans to move from one place to another. Although the Sun is millions of times heavier than the Moon, its effect on the tides is only half that of the Moon. That is because the Moon is much closer to Earth than the Sun is. The size of the tides also is determined by local factors, such as the slope of the sea bottom, the width of a bay, or the depth of a channel. For example, in shallow bays high tide may vary more than forty to fifty feet from low tide, while in the open ocean, the difference may be only a few feet. Although the tidal changes in the ocean are usually very gradual, in some places the tides are so great that you can stand on the shore and watch the water rising or falling as the tide comes in or goes out. Tides actually occur in all bodies of water, even small ponds. However, because ponds have so little water, the tide is so small it cannot be noticed.

In almost all areas tides occur twice daily. When the Moon is overhead, its gravitational pull causes the water on the beach to rise. It takes a little longer than six hours for the tide to come in fully (flood tide) and then an equal amount of time for the tide to recede to the lowest level of the day (ebb tide). A complete tidal cycle in most areas takes an average of twelve hours and twenty-five minutes. Because we have only twenty-four hours in the day, the times for the tides are about an hour later each day. For example, with high and low tides at 6:30 A.M. and 12:19 P.M., respectively, one day, the next day the tide would be high at 7:28 A.M. and low at 1:22 P.M. That corresponds with the rising of the Moon, which is also about one hour later each day.

Tide tables are charts published by the U.S. government that tell the time for the high and low tides throughout the year. For people who live and work near the ocean, the times of the high and low tides can be very important. The flow of water caused by the tide rising and falling can set up currents in some channels, making boat travel possible in only one direction at certain tides. Some areas may be too shallow for certain ships when the tide is out. In some harbors channels have to be dredged or dug out to enable boats to enter at low tide. And some shellfish can be harvested only at certain tides. For example, many mussel and clam beds are exposed only at low tide.

When the Moon is full and again when it is a new sliver, the Sun, Moon, and Earth are in a straight line. At those two times

Whitecaps and breaking waves batter the coastline during a storm.

in the Moon's cycle, the pulls of both the Sun and Moon are in the same direction, causing higher tides. Those tides are called "spring" tides. That name does not refer to a season of the year; it refers to strong, active movement of water that results in a larger tidal range. That means the water on the beach goes out and comes in farther than at other times of the cycle of the Moon. "Neap" tides have the smallest tidal range. They occur when the Moon is in its quarter phases. The word "neap" comes from Old English and means "barely touching" or "hardly enough." Neap tides occur because the Sun and the Moon are not pulling in a direct line, but rather at right angles to each other.

Some animals depend on the tide for their very existence. The grunion is a five- to eight-inch fish that lives along the coast of southern California. During the spring and summer months on nights of the highest tides, these small silvery fish lay their eggs on the sandy beaches. When the tide is highest, thousands of fish wash ashore on the waves. In an instant females lay their eggs, the males fertilize them, and the fish fling themselves back into the water.

It takes two weeks for the mass of eggs left behind in the sand to hatch. During that time they are undisturbed by the small neap tides. Each of the fertilized eggs hatches into a wormlike form, or *larva,* protected by a thin layer of moist skin, called a *membrane.* Just as the larvae are ready, it is time for another spring tide. As the flood stage of the tide occurs, the waves wash high up on shore where the larvae still lie buried in the sand. The cool water causes the membranes to break, and the small fish emerge and are carried out to sea.

Tides, waves, winds, and currents are the powerful architects of the coast. They constantly remind us of the difficulties in trying to predict weather or control nature. Having observed these natural forces in all moods and in every season, Henry Beston might not have felt betrayed during the great blizzard of February 1978. A spring tide coincided with gale force winds that howled along the Cape Cod coast. High-breaking waves battered the coastline, destroying some beaches and creating others with the washed-away sand. Extensive flooding occurred in low-lying areas. During the course of the storm, which continued for two days, Henry Beston's "outermost house" was swept out to sea.

3
Battle against Erosion

SCIENTISTS use the word "erosion" to describe the wearing away and breaking down of rocks and minerals on Earth's surface, causing changes in the landscape. The movements of water and glaciers are major causes of erosion. Perhaps you have heard about the erosion of topsoil from Midwestern farms and the erosion of sand from beaches. The former can happen suddenly, as the result of a storm. The erosion that occurs because of glaciers, on the other hand, takes place slowly, over thousands of years. Erosion is a natural process as old as Earth itself.

Geology is the science that deals with the study of Earth. Rocks, minerals, oceans, and caves provide clues to Earth's past. Scientists believe that throughout the history of Earth, periodic warmings and coolings of the world's climate have occurred. The intervals during which Earth became colder are called the Ice Ages.

During the last Ice Age to reach the continental United States, which occurred from two million to twelve thousand years ago, temperatures were very cold. The buildup of winter snow over many years was faster than the rate of summer melting. The snow became about two miles deep in some places. The weight of that snow caused it to change into ice and to form glaciers. Those slowly moving sheets of ice covered six million square miles of North America, including all of Canada, spreading over New England and reaching as far south as New York City and Long Island. The Greenland and Antarctic ice sheets are now all that remain of the last Ice Age.

Because so much ocean water remained frozen in glaciers and summer melting did not occur, the sea level was very low. It was as much as four hundred feet lower than it is today. The body of water now called the Bering Strait is believed to have been connected by a bridge of land that joined our present-day Alaska with Siberia. Ice Age mammals, such as the woolly mammoth, wolf, bison, musk ox, and reindeer, may have migrated across that bridge from Eurasia to North America.

Glaciers are one of the most powerful instruments of erosion. They work like giant bulldozers, scraping away tons of rock and soil as they move. You can easily see how that happens by taking an ice cube and rubbing it over the ground. Some of the soil particles and pebbles will be torn away and carried with the ice. Now put the ice cube on a concrete surface or even a piece of paper. When it melts, you will be surprised how much material it picked up.

About ten thousand to twelve thousand years ago, the most recent Ice Age ended in the continental United States. The

glaciers began to melt and withdraw to polar regions. In the activity you did with the ice cube and soil, the soil was left where the ice cube melted. In much the same way, glaciers carried tons of rock and soil from one place and deposited them miles away. Geologists call that process transportation and deposition. The kinds of material carried by the glaciers is called glacial till, a mixture of clay, sand, silt, gravel, cobblestones, and boulders.

Cape Cod was formed from glacial till accumulated from the scraping and grinding of glaciers as they spread over the layer of rocks near the surface of Earth—called *bedrock*—which exists in many parts of northern New England. When the glaciers melted, the deposited accumulation of earth and stones formed ridges or hills. The freshwater lakes and ponds on the Cape were formed from icebergs, large chunks of ice that broke away from the glaciers. Their great weight left large hollows in the land.

A sandy coastal plain extending from New Jersey southward is an example of an older beach. That wide stretch of light-colored sand was formed from the Appalachian Mountains. The mountains were eroded and ground down by the glaciers that covered much of North America during previous Ice Ages. Rocks and boulders from those mountains were crushed and ground and carried by rivers to the sea. During that journey they bumped against each other, were deposited in streams and riverbeds, and broke into smaller and smaller fragments. Some of them dissolved in water, some washed onto riverbanks, and

A glacier carves a notch in the rocky ridge and melts to form the lake below.

some eventually reached the seashore as sand. Grains of sand are made mainly of quartz and feldspar, two minerals worn from ancient granite rocks.

The West Coast of the United States is an area with evidence that much of our country was covered by water at an earlier time. When glaciers melted and the sea rose, it flooded places that had been dry since before the last Ice Age. Geologists have found the remains of marine plants and animals in regions that are now far inland. If you stand on many of the cliffs slightly inland from the Pacific coast, you can look toward the ocean and see terraces carved out by erosion. That level land was flattened by the ocean waves.

Along the California and Oregon coasts are short, narrow strips of sand, called "pocket beaches," between steep, rocky cliffs. They have formed from the grinding action of waves, which eroded the cliffs around them. When a wave crashes against a rocky cliff, the force of the water pushes air into the cracks and crevices of the rock. The force of that air enlarges cracks and causes rocks to break apart. As the waves continue to wash against the rocks, they break into smaller and smaller pieces and eventually become sand.

If you collect samples of sand from several beaches, you will notice that the sand differs in color and texture. That is because of the various material from which sand is formed. Sand with reddish purple patches contains specks of garnet. Most whitish yellow sand contains transparent crystals of quartz, a mineral found in rocks. The black sand found on many of Hawaii's beaches is made of eroded lava from volcanoes. In other places, such as beaches on the Florida keys, the sand is made mostly from shells or from coral that has been broken into tiny pieces. The individual granules of sand on different beaches have different shapes and sizes. Some sand is coarse, while other sand is so fine it feels like powder.

The smaller, lighter particles of sand are constantly moved by the waves, wind, and currents. They may gradually build up in one place to form a sandbar, a strip of sand that is usually underwater but becomes visible at low tide. With time, that may form a sand spit, which is a band of sand that extends from shore and disappears into the water. When a sand spit reaches across a bay, it is called a barrier beach. When both ends of a barrier beach are surrounded by water, it is called a barrier island.

Barrier beaches are long, wide strips of sand whose *land-ward* side is often bordered by sand dunes. The United States is fortunate in having one of the most extensive systems of barrier beaches in the world. Besides being excellent places to swim and boat, they are homes for fish and wildlife. As their name implies, they also protect inland areas from storms. Most well-known coastal resorts on the East and Gulf coasts are located on barrier beaches and islands. Some examples are Coney Island, New York; Ocean City, Maryland; Atlantic City, New Jersey; Virginia Beach, Virginia; The Outer Banks, North Carolina; Miami Beach, Florida; Waveland, Mississippi; and Galveston, Texas.

Barrier beaches are in a constant state of motion, which geologists refer to as "beach migration." The action of the waves rolling onto the beach gradually shifts the sand grains along the shoreline. That happens because currents that flow along the shore exist in many areas. The currents cause waves to roll in at an angle rather than exactly parallel to shore. Waves, constantly breaking at an angle, can move sand grains hundreds of feet along a beach in a single day. Violent storms

A barrier beach crowded with houses.

cause erosion, which is much more visible than the gradual shifting of the sand from waves and currents. A single storm can move tons of sand, ending the life of one barrier beach and creating another.

Sand dunes are continually being formed on barrier beaches. They are built by the wind and water. Wind picks up the dry

grains of sand and deposits them on the ground wherever it meets an obstacle—an existing sand dune, a row of trees, a snow fence, or something else. Layer after layer of beach sand builds up above the high-tide line. Gradually a slope develops, and a sand dune takes shape. It becomes so steep that grains of sand begin falling over the top to the landward side of the dune. As more sand accumulates, the dune slowly moves toward land, covering plants and trees that stand in its way.

Damage resulting from the natural process of erosion is more extensive now because we are using our coastlines differently than we did in the past. It is only within the past century that houses, stores, restaurants, hotels, amusement parks, parking lots, and paved roads have been constructed so

Sand dunes form when layers of beach sand build up above the high tide line.

close to the shore. As natural erosion occurs, it threatens our developed coast. In the future, the coast may be even more prone to erosion. Scientists believe that the temperature of Earth is rising. If that is so, the immense polar ice caps in Greenland and Antarctica may be in danger of melting. That would cause vast amounts of water to be released, significantly increasing the sea level. Coastal areas throughout the world

would be flooded, and erosion would occur at a much greater rate.

Some scientists believe that this twentieth-century global warming may not be due to natural causes, as in the past, but rather to human activities. We now burn much more coal, oil, and natural gas for energy than we did years ago. When those fossil fuels are burned, carbon dioxide and other gases and pollutants are released into the air. Although carbon dioxide is found naturally in the atmosphere, increased amounts of this gas cause more of the radiant energy of the Sun to be trapped in the lower atmosphere of Earth. The surplus carbon dioxide acts like a greenhouse, whose glass walls and roof trap the heat of the Sun inside. The trapping of heat, as a result of the production of carbon dioxide coming from burning fossil fuels, is called the "greenhouse effect."

According to another theory, our coasts are sinking because of natural changes on Earth. The outer layer of Earth is composed of "plates," which slowly move over the hot interior part of Earth. Uneven heating and cooling cause earthquakes, volcanoes, and the bulging of the surface of Earth in some places—and its sinking in others. Some scientists think that it is the sinking of land along the coast that contributes to the loss of beaches.

Our disappearing coast also may be due to the way we use the shore. When sand dunes are bulldozed to construct waterfront buildings or highways, or simply to improve a view, erosion occurs much faster than it would otherwise, because the sand dunes are no longer present to protect the inland

This road was washed out by waves and sand during a storm.

areas from the wind, waves, currents, and tides that affect the coast. Scientists estimate that, every year, parts of the Atlantic coast are losing an average of three feet of beach, while the Gulf coast loses seven feet a year in some places.

Some of the pocket beaches on the Pacific coast seem to be losing ground at the rate of about ten feet a year. This is in part because the sand on some beaches is not being replaced by natural forces. Erosion caused by flowing water creates sediment, which is deposited into streams and rivers and is then carried to the coast to form the pocket beaches. In southern California, many of those rivers have been dammed to create *reservoirs* for drinking water, or they have been diverted to supply water for crops and farms. As a result, the rivers no longer carry as much sand from inland areas to the coast.

Since the time of ancient Greece, two thousand years ago, people have tried to defend the land from the sea. Ancient Greeks built stone *breakwaters* to protect their harbors during storms. Breakwaters are structures placed offshore to spread out the energy of incoming waves. Modern people using sophisticated tools and equipment have improved breakwaters as well as designed other ways to restrain the sea. Fixed breakwaters are structures made of many different materials, such as stone or concrete. Floating breakwaters consist of materials that float between two anchors. For example, floating tires tied together may be held in place by chains attached to anchors or to wooden pilings. When a wave hits a breakwater, some of its energy is absorbed, lessening its force on shore.

Bulkheads and seawalls are structures that separate a bank or bluff from the sea. *Revetments* are graded layers of stone or other strong material extending uphill above the high-water

This revetment was built on the shore to protect the house above from ocean waves.

level. The rough, rocky surface of the revetment reduces the energy of the wave and prevents it from traveling far up the shore. *Jetties* and *groins* are structures that project into the water from the shoreline. Their purpose is to prevent sand from being moved by currents along the shore.

Now many scientists and engineers believe that all these costly efforts to preserve the coast are actually hastening its destruction. Building seawalls along barrier beaches has created what some geologists refer to as "New Jersey-ized

A groin helps to keep sand on one beach while depriving another.

beaches," beaches that have been carried away by erosion. Where once you might have put your beach towel on the sand, now there are only rocks and cobblestones, and in some places water comes right up to the seawall. At Monmouth Beach, New Jersey, a large boulder and concrete wall as tall as a two-story building was built to hold the beach in place. The wall, in spite of its size and strength, has not saved the beach. Instead, the sand has moved, leaving little of the beach remaining.

Seawalls and bulkheads bounce waves back without absorbing much of their energy. Waves then carry the sand offshore without bringing new sand in. Eventually that causes the beach to disappear. The foundations of buildings constructed near the water are weakened. Eventually they are unable to withstand the stress of the wind and waves during a storm and tumble into the crashing surf.

Other kinds of walls are often built to control landslides in areas where houses and roads are built on steep hills overlooking the sea. Because erosion is reduced, less material is loosened from the cliffs. Such soil and sand that normally builds up the beach is prevented from reaching it. It is another way that sand beaches are being lost.

Jetties and groins can create other problems. While they may, for a period of time, successfully trap sand moving parallel to the shore, they deprive areas farther down-current of sand. Parts of Waikiki Beach in Honolulu have been robbed of their sand by groins constructed up-current. In other places, such as Westhampton Beach, New York, the loss of sand caused by the use of groins elsewhere has resulted in the high tides coming in underneath many houses. Some houses have had to be elevated on supports to avoid water damage.

Instead of using methods to prevent sand from moving, some communities are trying to offset erosion problems with programs of beach nourishment. Sand is trucked in from the mainland or dredged offshore to replace what is eroded. Tourism suffers when beaches are lost, but replenishing sand is only a temporary solution. It is also very expensive. In the early 1980s, Miami Beach spent 65 million dollars to restore fifteen miles of beach.

Because there is such a high possibility of flooding and storm damage on barrier beaches, many private insurance companies will not provide coverage to people whose homes and buildings are located in certain high-risk areas. However, the federal government has spent billions of dollars to rebuild

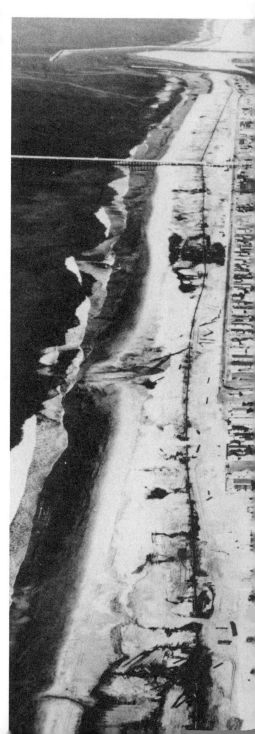

Two photographs of the same beach in Oceanside, California. The photo on the right shows the beach after 4 million cubic yards of earth were brought in to nourish it in 1963.

Houses built too close to the ocean may be destroyed during a storm.

roads and bridges and to provide flood insurance for those areas. The funds are often used to rebuild condominiums, hotels, businesses, houses, and other properties on the same sites where the damage occurred and where it will likely occur again.

With the passage of the Coastal Barrier Resources Act in 1982, the United States Congress designated 188 undeveloped barrier islands, spits, and beaches along the Gulf and Atlantic

Christmas trees stem beach erosion.

coasts as coastal barrier resources. Other barrier beaches were later added to the list. The act prohibits spending federal money to protect those undeveloped areas. Without any national flood insurance for protection, most people now will not

be willing to assume the financial risk of building in the vulnerable areas. However, the National Flood Insurance Program still protects thousands of miles of shoreline within coastal flood zones.

As the problem of erosion increases, people are exploring more effective and less costly ways of preserving beaches. Residents of Barnstable, a Cape Cod town, devised their own inexpensive solution to controlling erosion at Sandy Neck Beach. After the holidays they give this barrier beach a gift of old Christmas trees. People put their cut trees in the backs of station wagons and pickup trucks and into the trunks of their cars. When they arrive at the beach, they dig holes into which to place their trees. Even though the dead trees continue to drop their needles, the bare branches act as barriers against the blowing sand. Old dunes are built up and new ones are formed.

No matter what methods are used to control erosion, we must realize that they are only temporary measures. A groin may prevent sand from traveling down the coast, and a seawall may keep a cliff from tumbling into the ocean for a few years or maybe even a decade. But despite those structures, the forces of nature—waves, tides, and currents—will continue to be the powerful architects of the coast.

4

Pollution of Coastal Waters

~~~~~~~~~

POLLUTION is damaging many parts of our nation's coasts. Unlike erosion, which is caused by the uncontrollable forces of nature, pollution often results from the activities of people and our modern way of life.

One type of coast that is particularly subject to damage by pollution is an *estuary.* An estuary is a unique place where the fresh water of a river meets the salt water of the ocean. Over the years estuaries have become centers of human settlement. Inland goods were transported downriver to estuarine ports. Population increased, and busy harbors later grew into large eastern coastal cities—Boston, New York, Philadelphia, Baltimore, and Washington, D.C. Sewage and wastes from factories and businesses were discharged into the harbors. In many areas harvests of fish and shellfish sharply declined, and the

A seemingly quiet estuary teems with life.

water became so foul it was no longer appealing for swimming and boating.

Estuaries can be thought of as nature's mixing bowls. As the tide comes in, it flows partway up into the river, and as the tide recedes, the fresh river water flows farther out into the ocean. Currents and tides stir fresh water from rivers with salt water from the sea. Rivers flow to the sea, depositing sediment that contains sand, stone, mud, minerals, and pieces of plants and tiny living organisms. The incoming tide brings its wealth of contributions, including minerals, bits of seaweed, sand, shells, and sea, or *marine,* animals. The tide carries away much of the sediment. If deposits of mud and sand build up at the mouth of a river, they form a *delta,* which is a triangular-shaped piece of land.

Hundreds of estuaries exist along the coastlines of the United States. Many of them are so small they are nameless. Many of the larger ones are referred to as *harbors, bays, sounds,* or *lagoons.* Even some *fjords,* the long, narrow, steep-sided inlets of the Alaskan coastline, are estuaries. However, with the exception of fjords, the water in most estuaries is not deep. Sunlight can penetrate the murky water, reaching plants that grow on the bottom.

Salt marshes, like estuaries, are low-lying areas along the coastline, where the main plant life is salt marsh grass. In a salt marsh, however, there is no mixing of fresh and salt water as there is in an estuary. Nevertheless, salt marshes are extremely valuable areas that provide suitable places to live and food for a great number of species.

Most estuaries and salt marshes are difficult to explore on foot. The bottom is usually soft and mucky, covered with mud and sharp-edged shells. Rocks exposed at low tide are likely to be covered with slippery weeds. The air, which has a fresh, salty smell at high tide, may not be so pleasant at low tide, when there is the odor of a decaying mud flat. The nonliving rocks, mud, and air, plus the millions of plants and animals that live there, make up the ecosystem of the estuary or salt marsh.

The word *ecosystem* refers to a system of relationships that exists among living and nonliving things in a particular environment. "Eco" is derived from the Greek work "oikos," meaning house. A system is a group of things that forms a whole.

A coastal ecosystem is home to a community of plants and animals that have successfully adapted to that particular environment. In an ecosystem the energy of nature flows in a cycle. Therefore everything in an ecosystem is dependent upon everything else.

Nutrients and minerals from soil and water, as well as the Sun, enable green plants to grow. They produce food for animals and people, which cannot make their own food. Decomposers, which are *bacteria* and *fungi,* neither manufacture food, as producers do, nor eat it, as consumers do. Instead, they break down the bodies of dead plants and animals and return the nutrients to the water and soil. In order for an ecosystem to survive, its parts must be in balance. Because all living and nonliving things within an ecosystem are closely related to each other, pollution affects the entire ecosystem.

Because estuaries support such an abundance of life, they are some of the most important ecosystems on Earth. Tall, prickly rushes, reeds, and other marsh grasses grow in these valuable wetlands. Cord grass, one of the most visible plants, can live in water with different amounts of saltiness. It provides shelter for many of the animals that live in an estuary and food for insects and birds that eat its seeds.

Minnows eat young mosquitoes, and muskrats feed on cattails. Gulls swoop down to eat minnows stranded by the outgoing tide. Mink and raccoons have meals of clams, crabs, and mussels. Snakes hunt for frogs, and snapping turtles eat young ducklings. Mussels, clams, and oysters feed by pumping estuarine water through their gills, capturing minute dead plants and animals directed toward their mouths. Crabs and shrimp scrape food from the bottom. Some species of ducks, herons, teal, swans, and geese raise their young in estuaries. Without having to be plowed, seeded, fertilized, or weeded, estuaries

Chesapeake Bay, one of the largest estuaries in North America.

produce more food per square acre than do some of our most fertile farmlands. That is due in part to the fact that estuaries are nurseries for many of the ocean fish and shellfish we like to eat.

Chesapeake Bay is one of the largest estuaries in North America. Like many other estuaries, it is a "drowned" river valley. When the glaciers melted after the last Ice Age, the rising sea level flooded what had previously been a riverbed. Twelve major rivers, including the Potomac, Patuxent, Choptank, and Susquehanna, and about forty smaller rivers flow into the Chesapeake Bay. Its drainage area covers sixty-four thousand square miles, encompassing parts of Pennsylvania, Delaware, West Virginia, New York, Maryland, and Virginia. The watery arm of the bay reaches two hundred miles inland from southern Virginia to the port of Baltimore in northern Maryland.

For generations people have enjoyed boating, fishing, and camping in and around Chesapeake Bay. "Watermen," as they are called, have made their living by harvesting bay oysters, crabs, *finfish,* and clams. However, since 1950 the human population of the Chesapeake Bay area has nearly doubled. The beauty of this region has attracted people from Washington, D.C., and other nearby cities, and the population is expected to double again by the year 2020. Vacation homes have been built on former forest and pasturelands.

So many people using the bay so intensively harms the fragile estuary. The once-bountiful harvest of the bay is no longer as plentiful as it was. The harvest of oysters now is only one-third of that thirty years ago. Some shellfish beds have been closed because they have become *contaminated,* or unclean. Striped bass catches have decreased by 90 percent in the

The kind of boat and net used to catch hard crabs in Chesapeake Bay.

past decade. Marsh grasses also are dying. In their place are dense mats of algae, small water weeds floating on the water's surface, blocking the sunlight from reaching grasses that root underwater.

The changes in Chesapeake Bay are thought to be caused by pollution. Nitrogen and phosphorous, two elements found in chemical fertilizers, run off lawns and farms into the bay when it rains. They also enter the bay in wastewater discharged from sewage treatment plants. Those elements fertilize plants, promoting the rapid growth of algae. The algae take up oxygen dissolved in water, making the oxygen less available for other estuarine plants and animals. Sediments on the bottom of the bay absorb hazardous pollutants, such as weed and insect killers used on some lawns and farms. Toxic chemicals and metals formerly discharged into the bay by some industries in the area also cause serious contamination.

Today many people are helping to rescue Chesapeake Bay. Some farmers plow in a way that reduces erosion. That decreases the amount of silt worn away from the farmlands, which has buried underwater plants and choked clams. Less fertilizer also runs off the land. Less chlorine, which is used as a disinfectant, is discharged from sewage treatment plants. That will help increase fish populations. Citizen groups have educated bay residents about the proper disposal of hazardous substances, such as used motor oil, which in years past some people had poured directly into the bay. Laws have been passed that limit the amounts and kinds of waste that can be dumped into the bay.

San Francisco Bay is one of the estuaries most changed by human activity. The land around the inlets and marshes of that estuary located at the mouth of the Sacramento and San Joaquin rivers was inhabited by the Costanoan people when the Spanish soldiers and missionaries first arrived in 1796. The remote trading port of San Francisco remained small until gold was discovered in nearby Sacramento in 1848. Then the population jumped from about 400 to 25,000 in only one year. As the population boomed, gold mining, farming, and land development caused the estuary to change. Until 1884, gold was frequently mined by using high-pressure jets of water to loosen the sandy and gravelly sediments and release gold. The resulting rocks and mud blocked the streams and rivers, preventing some fish, such as salmon, from swimming upstream to *spawn.* In other cases sediments flowed down the rivers and streams into the bay. The sediments built up, causing the water there to become shallower. That resulted in changes in tidal patterns, which may have buried oyster beds.

With the completion of the transcontinental railroad in 1869, large quantities of live eastern oysters were transported by railroad car to San Francisco Bay. There they were buried in mud flats, where they grew to maturity and later were harvested. Along with the oysters, other species got a "free ride" and became established in Pacific waters. They joined the ranks of "introduced species," which means they were not native to San Francisco Bay, further upsetting the natural ecosystem.

In all, about one hundred *invertebrates* were introduced. Some of them, such as the eastern soft-shell clam and the Japanese littleneck clam, were sought after. Other species, such as the shipworm, are pests because they bore into wood, destroying wharves and bridges.

For years San Francisco Bay has been used as a sink for household sewage and industrial wastes. "Point source" pollution comes from the more than seventy municipal and industrial waste treatment facilities, which put millions of gallons of wastewater into the bay. Other wastes and pollutants enter it from "nonpoint sources." They include rainwater, which collects on streets, and water used for irrigation. Streets can contain traces of gasoline and motor oil and asbestos from brake linings. Rainwater carries those pollutants into the bay and contaminates its waters. Agricultural runoff may include *pesticides,* chemicals used to kill pests; fertilizers; and naturally occurring but toxic substances from the dry western soil, such as the element selenium.

Selenium in small amounts is a necessary nutrient for humans and wildlife. It becomes poisonous in larger quantities, though. In 1982 two species of ducks that live in San Francisco Bay were studied and found to contain high levels of selenium. Scientists suspect that fish and other wildlife may also have high levels of that element, which can be passed on to humans in food. Determining the effect of the pollutant on the wildlife of the estuary is difficult, but many scientists think that it is a serious problem.

The filling of San Francisco marshland to create dry land for farms, houses, and industries began in the 1850s and continued through the 1970s. Today less than 5 percent of the bay's original tidal marshes exist. Furthermore, the flow of fresh water from the network of wetlands emptying into the bay has been reduced by more than one-third. It has been diverted to provide an adequate supply of water for Southern California, which has little rainfall, extensive agriculture, and a large population. Because less fresh water flows into the bay, some species of marine life have been hurt by increased salt levels in the water.

Pollutants enter coastal waters in many other ways, too. Poorly functioning sewage systems located near the shore may cause sewage to leak into coastal waters. Boaters also flush sewage directly into harbor waters. In the last decade pesticides have been added to some paints used on the bottoms of pleasure boats and ships. The paints hinder the growth of barnacles and algae, which slow the speed of boats in the water. However, over time, salt water dissolves the paint, causing the harmful chemicals to be released into the water, killing valuable shellfish. Recently, however, the use of these paints has been banned on most boats less than twenty-five meters (eighty-two feet).

Plastics and other debris mar the coast.

Plastics are another major source of pollution. Since their development in the 1940s, their use has steadily increased. Think of everything you use every day that is plastic, from the milk jug in the morning to your toothbrush at bedtime. Unlike fifty years ago, if you walk along any beach today, you will find plastic litter. Although plastic products are convenient, their disposal has become a serious problem because most plastic is not *biodegradable.* This means it is not broken down by natural processes, but rather remains for hundreds and hundreds of years in the environment.

When nonbiodegradable plastic is disposed of on the shore or in the ocean, it can kill coastal animals. The National Oceanic and Atmospheric Administration estimates that one hundred thousand marine *mammals* and tens of thousands of seabirds die each year from eating or becoming entangled in plastic garbage. Styrofoam cups and cooler chests left on the beach are broken apart by the action of waves. Birds mistake the resulting bits of Styrofoam for clusters of fish eggs floating in the water. They eat the Styrofoam but cannot digest it. A plastic bag that earlier held a sandwich may blow out to sea, float on the surface, and be mistaken for a jellyfish by a hungry sea turtle. When swallowed, the bag can cause intestinal blockage and kill the turtle. Large birds and young mammals may get the plastic rings from six-packs of soft drinks around their necks. As they grow, the rings become tighter, causing difficulty in swallowing. Eventually they die of starvation.

Much of the plastic litter in the oceans also comes from dumping trash overboard from pleasure boats, naval ships, luxury liners, fishing boats, and other commercial ships. In

1987 the U.S. Congress passed the Plastic Pollution Research and Control Act. The law implements an international treaty to ban the ocean disposal of plastics from all ships within the waters of countries that have signed the agreement. The U.S. Coast Guard enforces the law in the United States' territorial waters.

Another type of pollution marred beaches along the northeastern coast in the summer of 1988. At that time medical wastes, including needles, bandages, and vials of blood,

This bird was a casualty of an oil spill in San Francisco Bay.

washed onto shores. Beaches had to be closed and resort areas lost tourist dollars because no one wanted to swim or boat in polluted water.

Oil is a major source of pollution of coastal waters. It comes mostly from sewer discharge pipes, normal *tanker* and shipping operations, and runoff from roads and other sources. Sometimes oil is spilled at sea as a result of the disastrous breakup of an oil tanker or an uncontrolled gush, called a *blowout,* from an offshore drilling well. The amount of oil that reaches shore depends on wind, waves, tides, and currents. Large amounts may blacken entire beaches. Sometimes oil attaches to solid particles and comes ashore as tar balls. If you walk barefoot on such a beach, the tar balls will form black, sticky patches on the soles of your feet.

A floating oil slick kills marine life. When birds land on the surface and dive into the water for prey, the oil coats their feathers and destroys their ability to fly. Otters' fur may become coated with oil, causing them to die because their coats can no longer insulate them from the cold, icy water in which they swim. Unlike whales and seals, they have no blubber to keep themselves warm. Some oil may settle to the ocean bottom and be taken up by plants and animals. Shellfish may then eat those contaminated species. Fish pass tremendous amounts of water over their gills and can absorb large concentrations of oil directly from the water.

When contaminated shellfish and finfish are unfit for market, fishing grounds are closed and people involved in the industry lose jobs. In Charleston Harbor, South Carolina, scum and a film of oil were fatal to crabs and many species of fish, such as flounder, mackerel, bluefish, and sea trout. The number of shrimp declined, and shellfish were no longer safe for people to eat. Similarly, before so many industries were located on the bay of Pensacola, Florida, on the Gulf of Mexico, shrimp, fish, and oysters were plentiful. People enjoyed swimming in the clear blue waters. However, with the inflow of wastes to the bay, its water became polluted. Fish died by the millions, and the playful porpoises, which no longer had a source of food, left the area.

While fish caught in clean, deep ocean waters are normally healthy, in some places the fish that live in polluted water have developed cancer. White croakers caught along the Los Angeles, California, shoreline, English sole caught in parts of Puget Sound, Washington, and winter flounder caught in Boston Harbor, Massachusetts, show evidence of cancer. When the fish feed, they take in some of the toxic pollutants as well and become diseased. Scientists are investigating whether eating contaminated fish can be harmful to people.

Although much remains to be done, in some places polluted waters are becoming cleaner. Stricter standards regulating the amount and kind of wastes that can be discharged into coastal waters were established by the Clean Water Act amendments passed by the United States Congress in 1977. As water quality improves, natural ecosystems begin to function again.

In Charlestown Harbor, the pipes that discharged raw sewage have been sealed off. A new sewage treatment plant purifies the sewage before the water is released. The scum and oil are gone from harbor waters. Shellfish beds that were closed for years are now reopened. Fish, shrimp, and shellfish are gradually coming back.

In Rhode Island steps are being taken to restore Narragansett Bay, which had become polluted by sewage, industrial wastes, and runoff from farms. In 1984 the United States Congress set aside money to study four major estuaries, including Narragansett Bay. The Narragansett Bay Project, as the study is called, has representatives from all the groups that have an interest in the bay—people who fish, factory owners, private citizens, government officials, scientists, educators, and environmental groups.

These groups and individuals are working together to try to determine how the desires of people who want to use the bay as a source of food, for recreation, industry, transportation, and even for waste disposal can be balanced in ways that will protect the bay. To do that, teams are studying the water entering the bay from point and nonpoint sources to see how it is affecting the ecology of the area. Rhode Island schoolchildren and their teachers assist scientists with their work aboard a research vessel. Using specialized equipment, they sample the sediment on the bottom and measure the oxygen content and salinity of the bay's water. In addition, they use nets to haul fish, crabs, and other marine life on board so they can be studied to find out if chemicals entering the bay affect these species.

Biologists (scientists who study living things aboard a research vessel) studied the decline of winter flounder by dragging a large, cone-shaped net along the floor of the bay to catch the fish. They attached bright orange, numbered plastic disks to the captured flounder and returned them to the water. People fishing in Narragansett Bay who caught a fish with orange tags could then provide helpful data by sending, along with the orange tags, notes telling how, when, and where the flounder was caught and its size to the Rhode Island Division of Fish and Wildlife. This helped scientists understand where the fish live, their feeding patterns, and other life processes. After this

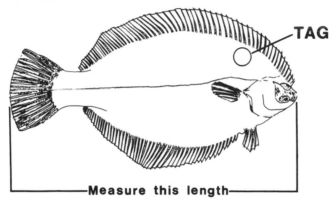

R. I. DIV. FISH & WILDLIFE
WINTER FLOUNDER
TAGGING STUDY

—TAG

—Measure this length—

HELP US STUDY WINTER FLOUNDER MOVEMENT.

PLEASE <u>RETURN TAG</u> WITH: DATE CAUGHT
LOCATION
FISH LENGTH
FISHING METHOD

<u>TO</u>: R.I. DIV. FISH & WILDLIFE
P.O. BOX 218
WEST KINGSTON, R.I. 02892
(401) 789-0281

R.I. Dept. of Environmental Management

This sign asks people to participate in a Narragansett Bay flounder study.

Students explore Narragansett Bay.

and other research has been completed, a decision will be made about regulations in the bay and how they can be changed to protect the bay's well-being.

Concerned citizens formed a group called Save the Bay to educate Rhode Islanders about Narragansett Bay and how to protect it. Now with more than ten thousand members, this nonprofit organization publishes a monthly newsletter, organizes conferences, speaks for the bay's interests at public meetings, and raises money to help support improvement of the bay. Profits from the sale of sweatshirts and T-shirts, mugs, and bumper stickers with Save the Bay slogans help to ensure that action will be taken to conserve this valuable resource.

Groups such as Save the Bay show that people can work together and be effective in stopping the problems of coastal pollution. You can help the work of organizations like this by becoming aware of the effects of pollution on the shore and by understanding that, like people, other species need a healthy environment in which to live.

5

Survival of Wildlife on the Shore

~~~~~~~~~

EXCESSIVE hunting and different ways of using the land forever changed the number and kinds of animals that, along with Native Americans, had lived on the coast since ancient times. When the *Mayflower* voyagers arrived in the New World, dense forests extended inland, and southern coasts had so many flowering plants that European sailors wrote about smelling the fragrance miles offshore. Deer, rabbits, wolves, bears, foxes, raccoons, squirrels, and many other mammals and birds lived in the woodlands. Mink and otter, opossum, wild turkeys, and bald eagles found food and shelter in salt marshes, meadows, and sand dunes. Seals, porpoises, whales, dolphins, and many species of fish were abundant in New England coastal waters.

Native Americans used the natural resources of the land and

seashore but did not use them up or destroy them. They hunted and trapped animals in the forests and used the skins and hides for clothing. Indian women gathered the wild plums, huckleberries, blueberries, mushrooms, mustard, and herbs that grew along the shore to use for food and medicinal purposes. They collected saplings (small trees) to use in constructing their wigwams and picked grasses and cattails to use for matting and weaving baskets. They saved the fluffy part of the milkweed pod to line moccasins and papoose boards.

Indians fished and farmed along the shore, and some tribes used horseshoe crab tails as tips for their fish spears. Native Americans originated what we now call a clambake. The men harvested lobsters, clams, and oysters. The women cooked the shellfish together with fish and corn in a pit in the ground over hot stones heated by burning logs.

Native Americans used the shells that they found along sandy beaches for many purposes in their daily activities. They used clamshells like spoons to scoop food from clay cooking vessels and birch bark bowls. The smooth insides of the shells of some periwinkles and hard-shell clams were used for making wampum, small beads used as jewelry and money. Sometimes those who held important positions within the tribe wore shells and colorful feathers.

In New England, Native Americans even used shells in farming. After clearing small patches of land in the forest, they plowed the land with hoes made from branches to which large clamshells were fastened with vines. Women tilled the soil and shaped it into mounds. In each mound they planted corn, pole beans, and pumpkin seeds. The beans grew up the corn stalks, and the large leaves of the pumpkin thwarted the growth of most weeds.

The Pilgrims had difficulty in adjusting to the conditions of the New World. Without the help of the Native Americans, they might not have survived at all. Native Americans taught the Pilgrims how to plant corn and how to make dyes and medicines from native plants. With that help and in spite of hardship and illness, the colonies grew. Eventually populations increased, and the life-styles the colonists had brought with them from Europe affected the natural coastline. They cut trees

Volunteers plant beach grass in an effort to reduce erosion.

for building boats and houses. They scrubbed wide pine boards with beach sand and used them for flooring. Marsh grasses became thatch for roofs, insulation in walls, stuffing in mattresses, and caning for chair seats.

Travel over land by ox cart destroyed plants such as beach pea, saltwort, dusty miller, sea oats, and beach grass, that grew in the dunes. Beach grass is tall and sea-green in color and has stiff blades with upright flowering spikes. Sea oats grow be-

tween two and four feet tall with small, flat clusters of seeds at the tip of their leaves. These plants are important links in the ecosystem because they are a source of food for birds and insects, which in turn are food for larger animals in the *food chain.*

Henry David Thoreau, a nineteenth-century writer and naturalist, imagined that if all the beach grass disappeared from Cape Cod, the ground would break up and the entire Cape Cod peninsula would be carried out to sea. He wrote:

"Thus Cape Cod is anchored to the heavens, as it were, by a myriad little cables of beach-grass, and, if they should fail, would become a total wreck, and erelong go to the bottom."

Beach grass reaches deep beneath the surface for moisture. It spreads by underground runners, and with time little sprouts grow in the formerly barren sand dune, which begins

Shorebirds (red knots) in the surf on the Florida coast.

to resemble a sparse field of wheat. The roots trap the grains of sand like fish in a net. Once the sandy soil is held in place, other plants that can live in sand also grow. Trailing beach peas, bayberries, sumacs, beach plums, pink and white wild roses, and scrub pines can be found in thickets along the dunes. Seeds from those plants are transported by water, wind, and birds in their droppings.

Native Americans had hunted and trapped some species of shorebirds for tens of thousands of years without threatening their population. However, ammunition brought with the colonists from England turned the work of hunting into a pleasure sport. In a brief few hundred years since the establishment of the Plymouth Colony, some species of birds were on the verge of extinction. The fact that shorebirds travel in flocks and nest and feed on open beaches or marshes

made them easy targets for hunters. Sometimes mass killings of birds were done just for fun and other times for profit.

Until the nineteenth century large flocks of shorebirds were common sights along sandy East Coast shores. Then it became fashionable to trim hats with bird feathers. Unfortunately, some of the most colorful feathers are grown only at *breeding* season.

Thousands of herons and egrets were shot by hunters who sold the feathers to hat manufacturers. With the passage of the Federal Migratory Bird Treaty Act in 1918, further killing of most species of shorebirds was outlawed. However, the numbers of some birds were already so low that they could not be saved. The great auk, a bird about the size of a goose, stood upright like a penguin and could not fly. It was shot for its feathers, and the bird and its eggs were eaten. The species gradually died out, and it is now *extinct.* Similarly, the heath hen was overhunted, and its numbers became so low it could not be saved. It, too, is extinct.

One of the shorebirds that lives along sandy beaches and is now endangered is the piping plover. This wading bird is between six and seven inches long. It is a sandpiper with a short neck and bill and large eyes. Around its neck is a black, broken "collar," and on its fore-crown is a little black spot. It has a pale, whitish breast, and its back is the same color as the sand. That color is a perfect *camouflage,* enabling the bird to fade into the sandy beaches where it lives. With its yellow-tipped bill, it catches insects on the shore, darting back and forth as it snatches up its food.

In the spring piping plovers build their nests on the sandy beach. They make little hollows in the open region below the sand dunes and above the hard, wet sand where only a few plants grow. The nests are lined with pebbles and pieces of seashells. Both parents take turns sitting on the dark and light brown speckled eggs until the chicks, which look like downy fluff balls, hatch. Some of the piping plovers' eggs have always been lost to predators (animals that live by hunting other animals for food) before they hatched. Gulls, skunks, foxes, and raccoons raid the nest and eat the eggs. As the populations

The piping plover.

of those animals rise, they become more threatening to the piping plover.

Human use of the beach increases just at the time the piping plover breeds and lays its eggs. People who unknowingly approach the nests may cause the parents to flee, leaving the nests unguarded and unshaded. The eggs or chicks can then become overheated from the strong summer sun and die. Another potential problem is that the eggs blend in so well with the sand that people accidentally step on them. Dune buggies and other off-road vehicles also crush the eggs. The birds, because they must compete with people for use of the coast, are often forced to build nests in less favorable places. During a storm the nests may be swept out to sea.

Besides shorebirds, other species living along the coast have sharply declined. One of them is the wolf. Wolves are the wild dogs of North America. If you are familiar with dogs, you could recognize much of the same types of behavior in wolves. When assertive, they stand stiffly with the hair on the back and tail raised and they may growl with bared teeth. When yielding, both wolves and dogs flatten their ears back and wag their tails. When submissive, they crouch. Wolves are loving parents, feed primarily on rodents and other small animals, and rarely, if ever, attack people. However, European settlers viewed wolves as enemies and offered bounties for killing them.

Since colonial times Americans have shot, poisoned, and trapped wolves to the edge of extinction. The negative attitudes many people have toward these natural predators persist today. Childhood tales, such as "The Three Little Pigs" and "Little Red Riding Hood," and even television cartoons cast the wolf in evil roles. Such vicious creatures exist only in the imagination.

Less than three hundred and fifty years ago populations of red wolves lived along the coast from southeastern Pennsylvania throughout the Southeast along the Gulf coast to central Texas. In recent years so few red wolves existed anywhere in the United States that in 1967 they were declared an endangered species. An endangered species is one whose numbers are so low that scientists think it may become extinct. In a last-ditch effort to rescue the red wolf from extinction, forty of the scrawny red wolves remaining in the wild were captured and transported to a special farm in Washington State. There, it was hoped, the wolves would reproduce and thereby increase their chances of survival. The pure-bred red wolf offspring, living in zoos, grew to adulthood.

Meanwhile wildlife biologists searched for a suitable place for the wolves to be reintroduced to the wild. The scientists wanted to find an environment where wolves used to live, where they could be monitored, and where people would not bother them. When the scientists were most discouraged because such a sanctuary did not seem to exist, the Alligator River National Wildlife Refuge in North Carolina was created. That area, one hundred twenty thousand acres of marshes and swamp forests, is a peninsula bounded by the Atlantic Ocean, the Alligator River, and a military reservation.

Realizing that myths about wolves exist, the project directors met with citizens to hear their concerns. Residents of the nearby Outer Banks were worried that news of wolves would cause tourists to stay away. Officials explained that the wolves would be fitted with special radio-controlled collars so the animals could be tracked twenty-four hours a day. If they left the land, or *refuge,* they would be captured and returned. Secondly, the officials explained that the caretakers of the wolves had tried to avoid forming relationships with them. That helped to ensure that the wild animals would remain naturally wary of people.

In January 1986, when the eight pairs of red wolves arrived at the wildlife refuge, many people were on hand to welcome them. Schoolchildren brought bags of pine straw, which they had gathered for the wolves' pens, and news photographers snapped pictures of the frightened animals. During their ten months in fenced yards, the wolves' diet was gradually changed from dog food to rabbits, squirrels, and raccoons killed on the road, and then to the live game that lives in the refuge. Six of the wolves seem to be thriving, but two females have died of infections resulting from injuries or illness. More red wolves have been brought into the refuge to replace those that did not survive. It is hoped that the females will mate with the lone males. If this and other similar programs are successful, wolf pups will once again be raised by their parents in the wild and the howl of the red wolf will again join the voices of the shore.

Today, laws have been passed to protect other species that may have been hunted to the point of becoming endangered. Since the Marine Mammal Protection Act was passed by the United States Congress in 1972, whales, walruses, polar bears, and other marine mammals are protected by law within our territorial waters. This area extends approximately two hundred nautical miles from shore. Before the passage of the law, some marine mammals were killed because they were thought to compete with the fishing industry for food. Others, such as

This red wolf is receiving a radio collar before being released.

some species of seals, were shot because their furs were valuable. Except for Native Americans, including the Aleuts and Eskimos living in Alaska, no one else has the right to harass, hunt, capture, or kill any marine mammal within the United States and its territorial waters. The act also states that except for those animals killed by Native Americans, Aleuts, or Eskimos living in Alaska, no marine mammal products can be brought into the United States. For example, if you bought even a small pin made of sealskin in a foreign country, it would be illegal to bring it into the United States and it would be taken from you at customs.

Despite the protection of that law, two methods of commercial fishing, trawling and gillnetting, kill large numbers of marine mammals every year. Both fishing methods use nets that are very effective in catching fish but are not selective in what they trap. Seabirds and large numbers of porpoises, dolphins, sea lions, and seals become entangled and die. By law, people who fish commercially are permitted to take a certain number of species that are incidental to their catch. Trawl nets, made of heavy twine, are dragged along the ocean floor and can capture more than fifty tons of fish in two hours. Gill nets can be miles long and are made of a kind of nylon that animals can neither see nor hear. When those nets are lost at sea, they continue to "ghost fish," with no one to empty the catch.

The supply of fish available for people and other animals to eat continues to dwindle. One possible solution might be to permit use of those nets only in very deep water. However, while that would be out of the range of sea otters and shorebirds, other species, such as porpoises, would continue to get caught. Perhaps the net should be shortened, the season limited, or maybe those nets should be banned altogether.

While overhunting and overfishing harms species, loss of *habitat* is equally devastating. The word "habitat" comes from a Latin verb meaning "it dwells." Habitat is the place or type of place where a plant or an animal naturally lives and grows. Pollution, construction of buildings and roads, off-road vehicles on the shore, and filling of coastal wetlands have affected the habitats of many species of plants and animals. When

Gill nets and trawl nets are often used to catch squid.

Off-road vehicles crush fragile nests and animals.

habitats are changed or destroyed, many of the native plants and animals cannot adapt to the new conditions and die.

As a beach-goer, you may be most familiar with coastal habitats and ecosystems in the intertidal zone. This is an area that is alternately covered and uncovered by the high and low tides. Its lower edge touches the open ocean, and its upper edge is bound by dry land. Within the zone species adapt to the ever-changing conditions of wetness and dryness.

The intertidal zone of sandy beaches is home to many animals that are so tiny or well hidden that we may not even notice them if we walk barefoot on the beach. At low tide only the top layer of sand is dried out by the warming sun. Many of the animals that live in the sand in this region are those that tunnel to where it stays cool and damp. Marks in the sand may be the only clues to the existence of a whole community of animals living underground. Tiny holes in the wet sand lead to burrows of the whitish yellow ghost shrimp. The pea crab (a small crab resembling a pea in size and shape) and the reddish scale worm frequently depend on the ghost shrimp to burrow out shelters for them. Other passageways in the sand are built by flat, greenish black worms, called lugworms, which are from three to twelve inches long. The lugworm feeds on decomposed plants and animals. Its castings, or excrement, are rich in nutrients and help fertilize the sandy soil.

The mole crab is an important link in the food chain between tiny plants and animals of the ocean and larger animals of the coast. The Pacific mole crab has a brown shell about an inch long, while the Atlantic mole crab's shell is pale yellow and about a half-inch longer. Large numbers of mole crabs burrow into the sand, which seems quiet and still as the crabs wait for the backwash of a wave to retreat over them. When that happens, the area suddenly surges with activity as the crabs "fish" by putting their feathery antennae into the water. As the mole crabs feed, they in turn may be eaten by fish, animals, or shorebirds.

When a bird population or any other part of an ecosystem becomes scarce, the entire ecosystem is affected. The plants and animals that are food of the endangered species become overabundant, and the predators of the endangered species must go hungry or search elsewhere for food. The balance of nature is very delicate, and because of the interdependency of each part of an ecosystem, any change in one part of it affects the total community.

Just as is true on long, sandy shores, a whole web of complicated relationships exists among plants and animals of rocky coasts. The cycle of life in the intertidal zone of these coasts depends upon the returning tides to bring in new nutrients and minerals and revolves around the dependence of one species on another. Crabs cling to the strong, swaying pieces of seaweed to keep from being washed out to sea by the surf. Sea urchins hide from hungry gulls in clumps of red Irish moss. Periwinkles eat seaweed scraped from the moist rocks.

A common sight on the intertidal zone of these coasts is rocks covered with barnacles. Many common barnacles are not bigger than your little fingernail, and thousands of them can live in a space the size of your beach towel. In large numbers they resemble a miniature lunar landscape covered with tiny craters.

When a barnacle is young, it attaches itself to a rock or other hard surface. Its body produces an adhesive cement that is so strong it is difficult to remove the barnacle even with a sharp knife. Within twelve hours of attaching itself, the barnacle

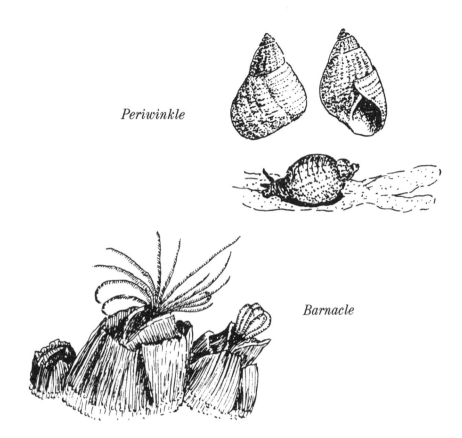

Periwinkle

Barnacle

grows a shell around its body that will protect it for its three-
to five-year life span. The cone-shaped shell has six outer
plates. When the barnacle is covered with seawater, the center
plates open. Feathery feeding parts extend through this hole
and act like a net, pulling in tiny plants and animals from the
water. At low tide, when the barnacle is exposed to air, the
"front-door" plates close, making a sound that one marine
biologist has described as the "whispering talk of the barnacles." If you visit the shore and discover barnacles, gently pour
a pail of water over them. You will see their "craters" open.

A tide pool surrounded by seaweed on a rocky coast.

On rocky shores tide pools form in the intertidal zone. Rocky crevices and hollows retain water as the tide recedes. Tide pools can be as small as a child's pail or as large as a swimming pool. Whatever the size, each tide pool is home to a community of plants and animals. Those inhabitants, unlike those that live in more typical intertidal zones, do not have to adapt to conditions of both wetness and dryness.

Low tide on a rocky coast is the time to discover the treasures of a tidal pool. Because life there continues just as if the high water had never left, we are able to get a close-up look at life in the ocean. The calm surface of tide-pool waters mirrors the sky, reflecting passing clouds by day and stars by night. Tangled masses of slippery, rubbery brown kelp frame it. This large, brown straplike seaweed provides shelter to a wide variety of animals that are tide-pool dwellers, including barnacles, starfish, crabs, sea urchins, anemones, and sea worms.

Sea cucumbers, another tide pool resident, somewhat resemble fat cucumbers with tentacles at one end around a mouth opening. Sea cucumbers move slowly in search of food on rows of tube feet on their undersides. They feed mostly on decomposed plants and animals. Sea cucumbers belong to the same spiny-skinned group of animals as starfish.

Starfish are also called sea stars because their bodies have extensions, or "arms," that resemble the shape of a star. Different species of starfish live along the East and West coasts. One of the most spectacular is the sunflower star, which is found in tide pools along the Pacific coast. It may be yellowish orange, reddish purple, or gray, and adult specimens can reach a diameter of two to four feet. On the underside of the rays, or arms, of all starfish are rows of tube feet that propel the starfish along. In the center of the underside is the mouth.

Starfish, which were briefly out of water for this photograph.

If at any time during its lifetime a starfish is injured and loses an arm, it simply grows another. A starfish's favorite foods are bivalve mollusks. They are soft, boneless animals with hard, protective shells composed of two movable parts. Oysters, clams, and mussels are bivalve mollusks. The starfish would not be able to eat the soft animal inside if it just put its mouth over the mollusk's hard shell. Instead, nature has equipped the starfish to pry the shell open. It wraps itself around its victim and attaches the suction cups at the end of its arms to the shell and pulls until the shell opens. It then turns its stomach inside out, inserts its stomach between the mollusk's shells, and digests the animal inside.

Tide pools and sandy shores of both the Atlantic and Pacific coasts are also home to hermit crabs, crabs that have soft outer skeletons. Their soft bodies, however, are coiled in shapes

much like that of a snail. Hermit crabs solve their shell problem by living in the abandoned shells of snails and other
animals. When the hermit crab outgrows its shell, it finds a
larger one. Perhaps the new shell belonged to a periwinkle,
moon snail, or whelk.

One species of hermit crab is sometimes found with a sea
anemone attached to its shell. Although anemones' tubelike
bodies and flowering heads look like plants, these creatures are
animals. By camouflaging the hermit crab, the sea anemone
protects it from enemies and in return gets leftovers from the
hermit crab's meal. Both animals seem to benefit from the
relationship. When the crab outgrows its shell, it separates
the anemone from the old shell and places it on the new one.

Tide pools are very special places. To explore their depths is
to become acquainted with the fascinating array of plants and
animals that live in these natural aquariums. People often
want to befriend these creatures and will put a sea cucumber
or hermit crab in a pail to examine more closely later. People
may not consider the harm caused the animal by moving it
from its tide-pool home. Usually conditions in the pail become
very stressful for the animal because the characteristics of the
ecosystem cannot be duplicated. Within the tide pool, temperatures vary naturally, as incoming tides cool the water, which
has been warmed by the sun. In a bucket, however, there is no
cooling tide. Then, as the water evaporates, the concentration
of salt increases in the water in the pail. That causes fluid to
seep out of the animal's body, and it dies. Tide-pool creatures
were becoming so endangered by collectors that, in 1971, the
state of California passed a law forbidding people to remove
plants and animals from tide pools.

Similarly, when snorkeling or scuba diving in tropical waters, people are often tempted to break off a piece of coral to take home as a souvenir. They are in awe of the beauty of this undersea world full of vibrant color and life swaying with the movement of the water. Starfish and sea urchins, brightly colored shrimp and crabs, yellow, green, and purple sponges, violet sea pansies and sea anemones, and brilliant red corals are anchored to other less brilliant corals. Lovely multicolored tropical fish, menacing barracuda, and perhaps a moray eel or a turtle might swim in front of your diver's mask. Everywhere are the exotic colors and shapes of coral reef creatures. But taking even a small piece of coral disturbs an entire ecosystem.

The builders of coral coasts are coral polyps, tiny marine animals. Like anemones and jellyfish, they have hollow, cylindrical bodies that have central mouth openings at one end surrounded by tentacles. The tentacles are armed with special stinging cells. When tiny animals float nearby, the waving tentacles touch and attach to the victim. Poison from the stinging cells paralyzes the prey. The tentacles carry it to the mouth, which is connected to the digestive cavity inside the body.

Stony corals and coralline algae, a kind of seaweed, are responsible for building coral reefs, which are hard limestone formations. These coral "cities" are ecosystems that are home to thousands of coral animals. Each species of stony coral builds its own characteristic colony. Colonies of brain coral resemble part of the human brain. Staghorn coral colonies have branching parts that look like a male deer's antlers, and needle coral colonies form thin, narrow stalks. Living among these hard corals are other types of corals. Soft corals have mushy bodies that offer little protection. Horny corals, such as sea fans and sea pansies, have flexible skeletons. Precious coral is a hard coral that can be polished and is valued for jewelry.

Coralline algae live in the crowded colonies and are a necessary part of them. The tiny plants give off oxygen, which the coral polyps require to live. They also use the nutrients in the animals' waste products to grow. Coralline algae make a limestone cement that coats the reef and holds the parts of it together. In that way the work of tiny coralline plants and animals can create reefs as large as mountains.

When a stony coral polyp dies, its body decays. However, its limestone "house" remains and forms part of the reef material. If the ecosystem is healthy, new polyps will continue to grow, often on top of the old limestone structure. The reef may also include mollusks, worms, snails, and other plants and animals.

Most species of coral live in shallow tropical water, where sunlight is most intense and beneficial to the coralline algae. The water temperature rarely falls below sixty-eight degrees Fahrenheit (twenty degrees centigrade). If you look at a globe, you can find this region. It circles Earth at its middle like a belt thirty degrees north and south of the equator.

Within the United States the coral coast is found only in the Florida Keys and the Hawaiian Islands. The Florida Keys, islands off the southern tip of Florida, were once living coral colonies. During the last Ice Age, about fifteen thousand years ago, sea levels had dropped so much that many coral plants and animals were no longer covered by the sea and died. About six thousand years later, with the melting of the glaciers, sea levels rose to their present height. The previously exposed coral reefs became a chain of low-lying islands called keys. Now living corals once again grow in these areas.

Like offshore coral reefs, swamps of mangrove trees, which grow along tropical coasts, teem with life. In the United States, mangrove swamps are found along the coast of Florida south of Cape Canaveral; the Gulf coast bordering Alabama, Mississippi, and Louisiana; and Hawaii. Because mangrove swamps are important wetland habitats and food-producing systems, they are thought of as the salt marshes of the tropics. More than fifty species of tropical trees and shrubs are called mangroves. The red mangrove, which can reach a height of eighty feet, grows closest to the sea. Next comes the dark, scaly barked black mangrove, mixed with the smaller white mangrove, which grows near the high-tide line.

Mangroves are the only trees equipped to live in salt water. Red and white mangroves have the ability to keep out much of the salt from the water entering the roots. Black mangroves absorb the salt water through their roots and then release the salt through special glands in their leaves. Sometimes white salt crystals can be seen sparkling on black mangrove leaves.

Because mangrove trees are water-bound, their roots have adapted so they can take in air. The red mangrove has "prop" roots that extend outward from the trunk through the air and then turn downward through the water to its bottom. This keeps the root in direct contact with the air over much of its length. Black mangrove roots send up slender, pencillike projections that extend above the water (except during the highest tides) and provide air to the roots.

Vast numbers of mangrove leaves continually fall into the tea-colored water, which is rich with decayed matter. The leaves, which are indigestible to most animals, are broken down by special bacteria and converted to protein. This, along with other decomposed matter, provides food for young shrimp, mollusks, crabs, and other invertebrates. They in turn are eaten by fish, birds, turtles, snakes, crocodiles, and people. Millions of tons of commercially important fish and shellfish begin life in mangrove nurseries.

Only recently have mangrove swamps been identified as important coastal ecosystems. In the past many people found these coastal jungles forbidding, with their dense overhanging vegetation and sparse sunlight. People viewed these humid,

Black mangroves with salt crystals on their leaves.

A small island of red mangrove trees.

mosquito-ridden swamps with thick, oozing muck underfoot as wastelands. They were used as dumping grounds for sewage and trash and drained to create dry land for building. In Florida, since the 1940s, hundreds of thousands of acres of mangroves have been dredged and filled.

An elaborate system of canals, dams, dikes, and ditches was built across south Florida to control flooding of property and

to drain land for agriculture. Now, rather than seasonal wet and dry periods, the level of water is regulated by steel and concrete gates. The absence of a natural wet and dry cycle caused by these engineered systems has brought many serious problems to the wetlands of south Florida.

That destruction and loss of habitat is affecting waterfowl that live in freshwater wetlands and mangrove swamps. Young ospreys may starve in the nest if the parents cannot find enough fish for them to eat. Many of the wading birds, such as herons and egrets, nest in mangrove trees. The wading bird populations, having recovered since the time their long, decorative feathers were used to adorn hats, are again declining. Now the reason is not hunting but habitat destruction. The declining number of the birds affects other species as well. Crayfish feed on fish eggs. By eating crayfish, wading birds help fish populations to increase.

The mangroves are home to a wide variety of endangered and threatened wildlife. Endangered species, those that are approaching danger of extinction in the wild, include the key deer, the Florida panther, and the green sea turtle. Wildlife is designated as being threatened when the population is likely to become endangered in the near future. Threatened species, such as the American crocodile and the loggerhead sea turtle, are carefully monitored to keep track of their numbers. Thousands of people visit the Big Cypress Swamp and Everglades National Park each year, hoping for a glimpse of the unusual mangrove animals.

Mangrove swamps are important to people as well as to wildlife. Their roots help stabilize the shoreline and help to build up dry land. During tropical storms heavily forested mangrove swamps protect the land from high winds and waves.

Today, in Florida, those swamps are increasingly protected by local, state, and federal governments. In the past some places with large areas of mangroves, such as northern Biscayne Bay, were destroyed for real-estate development. Recently proposals to fill mangrove swamps have been rejected because people are now aware of their importance.

The well-being of people and other species that live on the

shore is directly related. When we destroy coastal habitats, we are harming the land and water upon which living things depend. When the voices of birds and wild animals that dwell on the shore become faint, we need to take warning.

6

Coastal Rescue

~~~~~~~

ODAY more people than ever
before are becoming aware of the critical time facing the coast.
They realize that decisions made now will determine the future
of the nation's shore areas forever. Earnest debate about pollution of coastal waters, overbuilding on the shore, and the decline in wildlife is taking place. Not only did human beings
create most of those problems, but also, if they are willing, they
can solve them.

Out of the concern for the coast is arising a new group of
coast guardians who, like the official United States Coast
Guard, protects it. The official U.S. Coast Guard is a military
service that enforces the laws of the sea, called *maritime* law,
operates aids to navigation, and saves lives and property at sea.
Coast guardians are not part of any government agency or

organized group. They are identified, not by a uniform, but by a shared belief that the coast is a valuable resource that should be preserved for future generations. When you pick up litter on the beach, leave a sea cucumber in its tide pool, and forgo a beach buggy ride over fragile dunes, you are a coast guardian.

President Jimmy Carter was a coast guardian when, in his 1979 Environmental Message, he declared 1980 the "Year of the Coast." He stated that the "coastal challenge" was a huge task that called for finding the right balance between the nation's use of the coast for industry, recreation, housing, and business and the need for a healthy coastal ecosystem. That declaration resulted in the funding of a national effort to focus attention on the coast and to propose laws that could help protect fragile coastal areas.

When the Year of the Coast ended, another coast guardian, who was a leader in the Massachusetts League of Women Voters, wanted to find some way to keep the needs of the coast uppermost in people's minds. As a resident of Cape Cod, Barbara Fegan had seen how buildings displaced open land and how polluted shellfish unfit for market affected the local economy. She sent letters from her home and spoke before interested groups, proposing her idea that the Year of the Coast be followed by a yearly coastal celebration. From that grass-roots beginning, "Coastweeks" have become a nationwide annual event.

Held in autumn, Coastweeks are intended to provide an opportunity for coastal residents and visitors to learn more about the pleasures and problems of using the coast. Teachers, scientists, private citizens, environmental organizations, commercial fishing, and industries are enthusiastic supporters. Each year the number and variety of planned events increases.

They have included coastwide cleanups in Oregon, Washington, California, Texas, Massachusetts, and New York; trail repair on California's Point Reyes National Seashore; whale watches in New York; a lecture series on barrier islands in Georgia; a seaweed cookout in Florida; a nature walk to spot shorebirds in Maryland; and an art contest with a coastal theme in Massachusetts. The Coastal States Organization has named a Coastweeks coordinator in each member state. If you live on a seacoast or even on the coast of one of the Great Lakes,

A student using snorkel and mask observes sea life.

you can find out about Coastweeks activities in your area by writing to:

Coastal States Organization
Hall of the States, Suite 312
444 North Capitol Street, NW
Washington, D.C. 20001

There may be other projects under way that need coast guardians. For example, students in a town on the East Coast measured the sand along a three-mile stretch of beach. The purpose of the study was to find out if the groins and retaining walls that had been built were controlling erosion.

Students in math, earth science, marine biology, and shop participated. Shop students constructed five-foot wooden measuring sticks. Earth science and marine biology students measured the depth of the sand at designated points on the beach. Measurements were done every month in all kinds of weather when the tide was lowest. Math students entered the data into the school's computer and calculated how much sand had been gained or lost in each location. That information was then put on a graph to show the distribution of sand over a period of years.

If the town had hired an engineering firm to collect and analyze the data, it would have cost thousands of dollars. In recognition of the students' conscientious work, each student who participated was given a special award at the high-school awards ceremony in June.

In Seattle, Washington, a community-based Adopt-A-Beach program offers an opportunity for Puget Sound residents to be coast guardians. Puget Sound is an estuary with about 2,100 miles of shoreline. Almost two million people enjoy its beaches and fish and boat in its waters every year. In addition to being important for recreation, Puget Sound is a center of commerce and industry and is home to thousands of animals, including whales, shrimp, fish, and invertebrates. People who adopt a beach, a shoreline, a marsh, or an estuary do not have to be experts on the coast. All they need is a desire to play an important role in monitoring, preserving, and cleaning up Puget Sound.

Project coordinators from the Seattle Aquarium meet with individuals or groups who want to participate in the Adopt-A-Beach program. They provide assistance in planning projects, written materials for background information on the subject, and small amounts of money for the purchase of needed supplies and equipment. Students have carried out a number of projects. One school developed an exhibit of seaweeds, explaining their economic importance and the need to protect seaweed habitats. In another project children drew posters to call attention to the need for the proper disposal of household hazardous wastes so they do not contaminate coastal waters. One of the drawings was so effective that a printing company donated two thousand copies of the poster so it could be widely distributed. Teenage members of a 4-H Club collected shellfish, seawater, and soil samples for the county board of health so it could determine if the areas from which they were taken were safe for clamming. Elementary-school students and their teacher in one Seattle school wrote a play about coastal pollution entitled "Choices," which was shown on television.

Warning signs protect nesting shorebirds.

TERNS NESTING
THESE ENDANGERED BIRDS ARE HARMED
BY ANY DISTURBANCE

Keep Below High Water Mark At All Times

DO NOT ENTER
AREA BOUNDED BY SIGNS - PLEASE NO DOGS

Posted by Mass. Audubon Society Per Order Board of Selectmen

People who work for the United States Fish and Wildlife Service in coastal wildlife refuges are also coast guardians. The manager of the Parker River National Wildlife Refuge on Plum Island, Massachusetts, has had to withstand a storm of criticism for prohibiting people from using part of the beach. Every spring and summer this beautiful barrier beach attracts thousands of people who swim, sunbathe, and fish. Until recently, surf casters were allowed to drive along the beach from 6:00 P.M. to 8:00 A.M. during the fishing season. Now, in order to protect nesting areas of the piping plovers, half of the beach is closed. Managers of the refuge have put up tall fences to keep people out of nesting areas. Warning signs state Area Beyond This Sign Closed—All Public Entry Prohibited. It is hoped that with such protection of habitat, the decline of piping plovers will be reversed.

From the time the Constitution was written two hundred years ago and until recently, the role of the federal government relating to the coast has been limited to matters concerned with safe navigation and the national defense. Lighthouses, buoys, and other devices guided seamen, and coastal fortifications guarded the nation from intruders coming by sea.

The federal government began its involvement with preserving the coast with a National Park Service program to acquire land on the seashore. Before then, individual states had created seashore parks, such as Sandy Hook and Island Beach in New Jersey. In addition, some individuals and towns had bought and preserved the land in its natural state. The first national seashore designated by an act of the U.S. Congress was Cape Hatteras National Seashore in North Carolina. Since it was established in 1937, more have been created. Perhaps you are one of the more than 30 million people who visit the

national seashores every year. Eight are located on the Atlantic
coast: Cape Cod N.S., Massachusetts; Fire Island N.S., New
York; Assateague Island N.S., Delaware; Cape Hatteras N.S.
and Cape Lookout N.S., North Carolina; Cumberland Island
N.S., Georgia; and Cape Canaveral N.S. and Gulf Island N.S.,
Florida. Two are on the Gulf coast: Gulf Island N.S., Alabama;
and Padre Island N.S., Texas; and one is on the Pacific coast:
Point Reyes N.S., California. Congress has also created four
National Lakeshores on the Great Lakes.

Each national seashore has its own beauty and special fea-
tures. In Assateague National Seashore wild ponies gallop on
the barrier beach. Padre Island is a long strip of fine sand, and
Point Reyes is a rugged, rocky, fog-bound coast. National Park
Service rangers provide information, conduct nature hikes,
and ensure the well-being of visitors and native species alike.

In 1972 the United States Congress passed the Coastal Zone
Management Act (CZMA). The intent of the act is to protect the
coast by establishing a way that government, industry, environmental groups, and private citizens can work together to
develop a plan for managing the coast. The act is designed to
balance the need for coastal resources with the need to preserve
the coast for future generations. The CZMA is administered by
the Office of Ocean and Coastal Resource Management. That is
under the National Oceanic and Atmospheric Administration
in the Department of Commerce.

By passing the CZMA, the federal government for the first
time got involved with how land it did not own should be used.
Congress felt that it was in the national interest to encourage
states to preserve, protect, and wisely develop the nation's
coastline. Before that, land use had always been in the hands
of local and state governments. In order to make that more

acceptable, Congress said that participation by individual states was voluntary. In order to be eligible for federal money, though, states had to draw up a plan for managing their coasts.

Amendments to the CZMA passed in 1985 require states to reach certain goals in order to continue to receive federal

Students monitoring marine life along the shore.

money. One of the goals is to provide a way for the public to enter the beaches for recreation. Now many people are prevented from using beaches because of lack of public rights of way. Another goal of the act is to reduce erosion and protect dunes, barrier beaches, islands, estuaries, and other wetlands from destruction. The goal of preserving the coast must be balanced with other national needs. For example, when offshore drilling is proposed, the need for oil must be weighed against the possible harmful effects of water pollution resulting from normal drilling operations or a blowout, if it should occur.

The CZMA also provides assistance for restoring city waterfronts. Some of them have been converted into thriving and attractive parts of a city. Rotting wharves and dilapidated buildings have been replaced by waterfront parks, new developments, and festival marketplaces. Festival markets, such as Boston's Faneuil Hall Marketplace, Norfolk's Waterside, San Francisco's Ghirardelli Square, Baltimore's Harborplace, and Miami's Bayside, have helped to restore pride in city shorefronts and bring in millions of tourist dollars. Seaside specialty food and clothing shops, hotels, restaurants, musical events, art shows, and live performances provide a festival atmosphere. However, when festival markets are being planned, citizens must make sure that land is set aside for pleasure as well as for profit. Such things as jogging paths, bikeways, picnic areas, and open space for wildlife should be part of the plan.

The National Estuarine Sanctuary Program was established as part of the CZMA. It provides money to help states purchase and manage estuaries within their borders. Since 1974, twelve large wetland areas totaling 243,376 acres and representing

different kinds of estuarine habitats have been established. The first National Estuarine Sanctuary was South Slough in Coos Bay, Oregon. Rookery Bay, Florida, is an 8,500-acre sanctuary that was created primarily to preserve a mangrove swamp. The purpose of the National Estuarine Sanctuary Program is to gain a better understanding of what life in the estuary is and how human activities affect the plants, animals, and nonliving things that are part of those valuable ecosystems. Efforts are being made to bring back wildlife to estuaries located near cities. Thirty widely different islands in Boston Harbor, some of which have in the past served as waste disposal sites and homes for the poor and diseased, became a state park in 1970. Easily reached by tour boat, some islands such as George's Island with its large Civil War fort, are rich in history, some offer the fun of wild berry picking and picnicking, and some are wilderness areas. Within sight of the city's high-rise buildings, black-crowned night herons raise their young, foxes tunnel through brush to their dens, glossy ibis and barn owls nest, and muskrats build their lodges. As the water in Boston Harbor is cleaned up with improved sewage treatment, it is hoped that the number and variety of wildlife species will steadily increase in this urban estuary.

If you live near an estuary, call your state Office of Coastal Zone Management to find out what plans have been made for it. Are measures being taken to control development and pollution? Write to public officials, letting them know of your interest. Ask to be sent a list of your state's estuaries with

Faneuil Hall Marketplace, Boston, Massachusetts.

information about the people and agencies responsible for managing them.

In a democracy such as we have in the United States, citizens are the decision makers. Elected officials want to know what future voters think about coastal issues. Write to them to let them know your thoughts. Request information from them, so that you can keep informed on coastal matters.

Decisions that had been made in the past regarding our use of the coast were often made without much thought of long-term consequences. The coast seemed to be so resilient that it could take care of itself and even recover from misuse. However, we have learned that dumping tons of garbage into harbors, filling salt marshes, or drilling for offshore oil—while helping to solve immediate problems—often created many others for the coast.

The great increase in human population on our nation's shores and the ways we have used these areas have caused most of the coast's problems. Just as we use this valuable resource much differently than the Pilgrims did, future generations will use the coast in ways we can only guess at today. We must remember that coastal ecosystems are not just a collection of plants, animals, and minerals. They are complex living communities in which complicated relationships exist. When people mismanage the coast, the changes affect many species on Earth. We know more about the coast than any society has ever known, and we must heed its call for help. As a future coast guardian, perhaps you will lead the way toward preserving this irreplaceable natural resource.

GLOSSARY

Bacteria—One-celled organisms that live in soil, water, air, or living things. They are so tiny that they can be seen only with a microscope.

Bays—The parts of a sea or lake that stretch into the land, usually smaller than a gulf.

Bedrock—A layer of unbroken solid rock covered in most places by soil.

Biodegradable—Capable of being broken down into harmless products by the action of decomposers.

Biologists—Scientists who study living things.

Blowout—An uncontrolled gush of oil from oil drilling operations.

Breakwaters—Structures placed offshore to spread out the energy of incoming waves.

Breeding—The producing of young.

Bulkheads—Walls or embankments to protect the shore from erosion.

Camouflage—A disguise or false appearance that is used to hide something.

Contaminated—Made impure or dirty by soiling, staining, or infecting by contact.

Currents—Parts of the air or a body of water, which move along in a certain direction.

Delta—An area of land at the mouth of a river, formed by deposits of earth, sand, and stone. A delta is usually shaped like a triangle.

Dunes—Mounds or ridges of sand that have been piled up by the wind.

Ecosystem—A system of relationships that exist among living and nonliving things in a particular environment.

Environment—The air, land, water, and all living and nonliving things that make up a certain place.

Erosion—A slow wearing, washing, or eating away by the action of wind, water, or glacial ice.

Estuary—A place along the coast where the fresh water of a river meets the salt water of the ocean.

Extinct—No longer existing, no longer active.

Finfish—A fish having fins, as distinguished from a shellfish.

Fjords—Narrow inlets or arms of the sea bordered by steep cliffs, especially in Norway.

Food chain—Order of organisms in which each uses the next, usually lower, member of the order as a food source.

Fungi—A group of plants that, like bacteria, cannot make their own food. Fungi include yeast, molds, and mushrooms. They aid in the decay of dead plants and animals.

Geology—The science that deals with the natural history of Earth through examination of its rocks and minerals.

Glaciers—Large masses of ice formed by snow that does not melt. They move slowly down a valley or across land.

Gravitational—Of or relating to the force or pull that draws all bodies in the universe toward one another.

Groin—A small jetty extending from shore to prevent beach erosion.

Habitat—The place where a plant or an animal naturally lives and grows.

Harbors—Sheltered places along the coast.

Invertebrates—Animals that do not have backbones, such as sponges, worms, insects, and lobsters.

Jetties—Walls built out of rocks, wood, concrete, or steel that extend into a body of water. They are used to protect a harbor or offset a current.

Lagoons—Small pondlike bodies of water that open onto larger bodies of water.

Landward—Living or being on the side toward the land.

Larva—An insect in its earliest stage of development after it has hatched.

Mammals—Animals that are warm-blooded and have a backbone. The females have glands that produce milk for feeding their young.

Marine—Having to do with the sea.

Maritime—Of or relating to navigation or shipping on the sea.

Membrane—A thin layer of moist skin or tissue.

Moors—Open areas of wild land with few trees, which are often wet and spongy.

Natural resources—Living and nonliving things found in nature, which are valuable or useful for people's lives.

Nutrients—Substances needed by living things to survive.

Pesticides—Chemicals used to kill pests.

Pollution—Something that causes an unclean or impure state.

Refuge—A shelter or protection from danger or trouble.

Reservoirs—Natural or artificial lakes used to store drinking water.

Revetments—Graded layers of stone or other strong material extending uphill above high-water level.

Salinity—Saltiness.

Salt marshes—Flat lands on which flooding by salt water occurs.

Seawalls—Walls or embankments to protect the shore from erosion.

Sewage—The total of bodily wastes and wastewater produced by residences, farms, businesses, and industries.

Shellfish—Water-dwelling invertebrate animals with shells.

Silt—Very fine particles of sand, clay, dirt, and other material carried by flowing water.

Sounds—Wide channels linking two large bodies of water or separating an island from the mainland.

Spawn—To produce or deposit eggs.

Tanker—A ship fitted with tanks in which oil or other liquids can be carried.

Wastewater—Water carrying dissolved or suspended solids from homes, farms, businesses, or industries.

SOURCES OF MORE INFORMATION

Adopt-A-Beach Program
The Seattle Aquarium
Pier 59
Waterfront Park
Seattle, Washington 98101

American Littoral Society
Sandy Hook
Highlands, New Jersey 07732

Coast Alliance
218 D. Street, SE
Washington, D.C. 20003

Coastal States Organization
Hall of States, Suite 312
444 North Capitol Street, NW
Washington, D.C. 20001

Defenders of Wildlife
1224 19th Street, NW
Washington, D.C. 20036

Florida Audubon Society
1101 Audubon Way
Maitland, Florida 32751

Greenpeace
1611 Connecticut Avenue, NW
Washington, D.C. 20009

National Sea Grant Program
6010 Executive Boulevard, W.S.
C-5
Rockville, Maryland 20852

Natural Resources Defense Council
122 East 42nd Street
New York, New York 10168

Office of Ocean and Coastal
    Resource Management
3300 Whitehaven Street, NW
Washington, D.C. 20235

Save the Bay
434 Smith Street
Providence, Rhode Island 02908

Sierra Club
730 Polk Street
San Francisco, California 94109

Woods Hole Oceanographic
    Institution
Woods Hole, Massachusetts 02543

SUGGESTED FURTHER READING

Books for Young People

Blassingame, Wyatt. *Wonders of Egrets, Bitterns, and Herons.* New York: Dodd, Mead & Company, 1982.

Bramwell, Martin. *Oceans.* New York: Franklin Watts, 1984.

Coburn, Doris. *A Spit Is a Piece of Land.* New York: Julian Messner, 1978.

Couffer, Jack, and Mike Couffer. *Salt Marsh Summer.* New York: G. P. Putnam's Sons, 1978.

Epstein, Sam, and Beryl Epstein, with Michael Salmon. *What's for Lunch? The Eating Habits of Seashore Creatures.* New York: Macmillan Publishing Company, 1985.

Gallant, Roy A. *The Ice Ages.* New York: Franklin Watts, 1985.

Johnson, Sylvia A. *Coral Reefs.* Minneapolis: Lerner Publications Company, 1984.

Johnson, Sylvia A., and Alice Aamodt. *Wolf Pack.* Minneapolis: Lerner Publications Company, 1985.

Lambert, David. *The Oceans.* New York: Franklin Watts, 1984.

Malnig, Anita. *Where the Waves Break: Life at the Edge of the Sea.* Minneapolis: Carolrhoda Books, Inc., 1985.

McClung, Robert N. *Hunted Mammals of the Sea.* New York: William Morrow and Company, 1978.

Padget, Sheila. *Coastlines.* New York: The Bookwright Press, 1984.

Pringle, Lawrence. *Estuaries: Where Rivers Meet the Sea.* New York: The Macmillan Company, 1973.

Robin, Gordon de Q. *Glaciers and Ice Sheets.* New York: The Bookwright Press, 1984.

Schreiber, Elizabeth Anne. *Wonders of Terns.* New York: Dodd, Mead & Company, 1978.

Schreiber, Elizabeth Anne, and Ralph W. Schreiber. *Wonders of Sea Gulls.* New York: Dodd, Mead & Company, 1975.

Sheperd, Elizabeth. *Tracks Between the Tides.* New York: Lothrop, Lee & Shepard Co., 1972.

Silverberg, Robert. *The World Within the Tidal Pool.* New York: Weybright and Talley, 1972.

Stephens, William M. *Life in a Tide Pool.* New York: McGraw-Hill Book Company, 1975.

Other Books

Beston, Henry. *The Outermost House.* New York: The Viking Press, 1928, 1964.

Jackson, Thomas C., ed. *Coast Alert: Scientists Speak Out.* Stamford, Conn.: Oceanic Society, 1981.

Kaufman, Wallace, and Orrin Pilkey. *The Beaches Are Moving.* Garden City, New York: Anchor Press, Doubleday, 1979.

Simon, Anne W. *The Thin Edge.* New York: Harper & Row Publishers, 1978.

Articles

Carey, John. "Mangroves . . . Swamps Nobody Likes." *International Wildlife* (September–October 1982): 21–28.

"The Coast." *Oceanus* (Winter 1980/1981): entire issue.

"The Dirty Seas." *Time* (August 1, 1988): 44–50.

"Our Troubled Coasts." *Oceans* (March–April 1987): entire issue.

Platt, Rutherford H. "Congress and the Coast." *Environment* (July–August 1985): 12–17.

Rudloe, Anne, and Jack Rudloe. "The Changeless Horseshoe Crab." *National Geographic* (April 1981): 562–72.

Wiley, John P. "On Tropical Coasts, Mangroves Blend the Forest into the Sea." *Smithsonian* (March 1985): 122–35.

INDEX